ADRIAN'S BLIGHT

BY
PHILLIP TUCKER

WWW.PHILLIPTUCKER.COM.AU

ACKNOWLEDGEMENT

To my family and friends. As long as a man has both, he is truly blessed. Thanks to all of you for your support. A special thanks to Steven and Dianne.

COPYRIGHT © PHILLIP TUCKER 2013

Cover illustration and design copyright to Lindsey Bidwell at Bidwell Media, visit: www.bidwellmedia.com.au

CONTENTS

PRESENT DAY AMERICA

Light soaked into Brett's thundering migraine, waking him. His eyes screaming out soundlessly, trying to focus, on the dim orange glow that filled his vision. He knew he was face down, his hands extended, but not much else. Moving his fingers, he felt what could be either carpet or grass, though he couldn't be sure. Trying to rise, he felt his muscles tense, then collapse, as they caved in refusing to function.

"What the fucks going on?' he asked himself as the orange glow intensified. Summoning strength through fear, he managed to move his tongue wetting his parched lips. Instantly his tongue retreated, as the foul taste of vomit made his body maliciously respond. In three shuddering heaves, it tried unsuccessfully to cast out the remainder of his stomach. Pain knifed through his head as the orange glow persisted, scaring him, making his limited supply of adrenalin surge into his nervous system.

"God don't let me be blind." He sobbed as his hands hesitantly moved towards his eyes. Fearing the worst, his trembling fingers searched, finding something stuck over to his forehead. With a monumental effort, he pulled the hideous light-sucking creature from his face. Light, beautiful, clean light, bathed him in hope, expelling his fear, as he pulled the object free. Pain again struck him as the pure light replaced the orange creature, stabbing his slowly recovering brain. Blinking, focusing, Brett unwillingly looked at his orange tormentor. A McDonald's hamburger wrapper stared back at him.

Cursing, he screwed it up, hurling it away from him, as his arms again started functioning. This allowed him the luxury of wiping his hands on his shirt, cleaning off what remained of his meal. To his horror, they came away wet, from the pool of urine he was lying in. Disgusted he pushed himself off the floor, getting into a sitting position, while still holding his head between both his hands. Through the pain, he started to shiver, as the cold penetrated through his minds fog, his body gradually awakened.

"What the hell happened to me?" He whimpered, disorientated. His imagination told him that some delusional person or creature unknown had drugged and kidnapped him. Shaking with both cold and terror, he pondered what sordid and perverted punishment had already been inflicted on him. Petr fied, he slowly looked around at his surroundings, trying to work out where he'd been taken. Beside him, lying dejectedly on the floor, he glimpsed his tormentor. An empty bottle of Jack Daniels.

"So that's what happened." He groaned the memory of the day before breaking through his latest binge.

He'd awoken that morning like today, with a hangover. Staggering out of bed at 9, he remembered he had an interview for a night watchman's job at 11. He recalled hazily, showering and shaving, before dressing. Clean clothes he found were in short supply, so he opted for a dirty shirt from another interview from the day before. Removing his pants from under the bed's mattress, where he'd left them to flatten out; he put them on, before searching for his coat.

At first, he thought he'd lost it, having gone through all his closets. Walking through to the driving section of the RV he found it hanging near the steering wheel. How it got there, he had no idea, although he briefly remembered in his last session of binge drinking, trying to start the RV. Happy he'd found it, he put on his slightly crumpled jacket.

Looking in the mirror, he saw a guy who still looked good. The suit though not the best gave him a presentable look. The bloodshot eyes, unfortunately, betrayed what he'd become. Feeling his hand start to shake, he decided on a drink to steady his nerves.

"Just one, that's all I'll need," he assured himself. Opening a fresh new virgin bottle of the Jack, he filled the bottle cap with a nip of paradise. Swallowing it in one gulp, he felt the liquid slide down his throat, tantalising his taste buds, calming every fear. One hadn't been enough, so he'd knock back another. After several pick me ups, he decided to stay home.

"Screw the interview. Who'd the fuck wants to be a fucking night-crawler anyway?" He'd laughed, enjoying his flight from reality.

Now he lay in the aftermath of his bravado, trying to remember what had happened to another day and night. Crawling to his bed, he inched up onto it, off the floor. The RV he lived in was trashed beyond repair. Looking down at his clothes he realised he was still in his suit. Now, like himself, it was wasted. Lying down, he stared at the ceiling, passing out.

Coming around, seeing the sun was fading, he sat up. His head at least had stopped thumping. Searching through the RV's littered floor, he located a bottle of Jack with a nip full of happiness still intact. As if finding a religious artefact he reverently unscrewed the lid, downing it in one swallow. Partially revived he staggered to his feet, scratching his wet smelly crotch. Stripping down, he removed his urine soaked underwear and pants, then his shirt. Tossing them into an overflowing clothes hamper, he searched for something to wear.

Finding a pair of old shorts and of all things a turtleneck pullover he gathered a towel and some soap.

Ready, he kicked his way through the rubbish littered floor moving outside. Connected to his RV by a sheet of plastic was an outhouse, which contained his toilet and shower. Needing a piss, he got straight into the shower, killing two birds with one stone. Turning on the water, urinating at the same time, he waited for the arrival of the hot water. Finished relieving himself, he continued to wait for the hot water, when a piece of paper, caught his attention.

Pinned to the shower door was a formal eviction notice, telling him in legal terms to fuck off. It also mentioned the power and hot water had been turned off. Cursing everyone he could think of past and present, who'd ever done him wrong, he admitted defeat, moving under the cold water. It was freezing, causing another outbreak of blasphemy against any God who had dared to put him on this God forsaken planet. Settling down, coming to terms with the arctic water, Brett slowly applied the soap to his filth-covered body.

After putting up with the deluge of frozen water for several agonising minutes, Brett considered himself clean enough after his latest binge. Finding at least the towel worked, he dried himself, turning off the still flowing glacier next to him. Remorse gripped him, as it occurred to him that again he'd pissed off a chance to get a job.

Since being fired from the agency, he'd spiralled down from his usual depressed outlook to absolute misery. When he'd been kicked out, Linda the only friend he had left suggested he hire himself out as a bodyguard. She even set up a website, putting a glossy photo of him from better days on the site. Despite his doubts, he'd been hired twice.

Unfortunately, both customers had a 'don't turn up so drunk you can't stand up' policy. In other words, he'd been canned from both assignments. Since then the phone had stopped ringing, having been cut off. Now facing eviction from this shithole, he saw nothing ahead except living on the streets. Even Linda had given up on him, after the two jobs fiasco. She'd left for who knows where.

"Who could blame her?" Brett murmured admitting to himself, that he'd failed her.

Back inside the RV, disgusted with the pigsty he'd been living in, he tried to clean the van up. Tired and overwhelmed by the amount of rubbish, he, in the end, gave up. Boiling some water instead, he decided on a cup of coffee to lift his mood. At least the gas still worked he smiled, getting a rare good mood swing from his dilemma. Finding his still working watch under the bed, he discovered it was just past 2 in the afternoon. That gave him the rest of the day and till lunchtime tomorrow to be packed and out.

Sitting there, Brett toyed with the idea of making a run for it in the RV, rather than lose it. Checking to see if it would start, he noticed the fuel tank was empty, compliments of the park owner.

"The bastard thought of everything." Brett chuckled.

Feeling hungry Brett looked around for something to eat. Finding some crackers only half stale, he gobbled them down, feeling replenished. Continuing to dig, he hit the jackpot, finding a can of beans. Getting out a can opener he swiftly cut off the can lid. With no spoon in sight, he guzzled down the contents while sipping his coffee.

"Well, I'll worry about packing tomorrow," he told himself, continuing to sip the sugarless black mixture, trying to think of a solution. A loud bang on his door made him jump, spilling his black gold.

"Who is it? What the fuck do you want?" He screamed, his good mood evaporating as he hastily stripped of his drenched coffee pants before his manhood was burnt off.

"Fed Ex. We've got a delivery for a Mister B Heckle of Heckle Private Detectives." At first, Brett thought it was a joke, till he remembered that it was the name of the bodyguard firm Linda had set up.

"Okay, I'll be right there," Brett answered hobbling to the door. Moving outside, Brett watched the Fed Ex guy shift backwards, staring at him. He had to admit he looked a little unhinged in his present attire.

"You're Heckle Private Detectives?" The guy asked obviously expecting someone else, like a human.

"Yes, I am. So hand it over!" Brett snarled.

"Have you got some kind of ID?"

"I've got a gun around here somewhere, it belongs to the business. Would that do?" Reluctantly the Fed Ex man handed over a large envelope, asking for a signature instead. Signing quickly, Brett gave him a lukewarm thanks, before heading back inside.

"Fucking loser!" Brett heard the guy shout from a distance, as he swiftly fled, having a happy moment at Brett's expense.

Once inside, and having no power, he pulled open the curtains so he could see clearly. The windows were so filthy he was forced back outside so he could check out his delivery. Tearing open the envelope he saw three things. The first was an open first class ticket to New Zealand. The second was a bank cheque for ten grand, the third a sealed letter. Intrigued and to say the least and a little wary, Brett opened the letter.

It was an offer for employment to protect a businessman in the diamond trade. He'd had a few threats and seeing Brett had a history of employment in the FBI, asked if he would come out to his home for an interview. Brett sat there for the next few minutes unable to do anything, before bursting into uncontrollable laughter.

"Wholly shit someone believed that bullshit Linda wrote!" He screamed, wiping tears from his eyes. His first thought was to head for the bottle shop, cash the cheque and have one halleluiah of a party. Staring at the cheque his smile left his face, as a chance to salvage something of his life occurred to him. 'Could he do it?" was the question, as he sat silently contemplating his chances of success?

In the end, he came to the conclusion, that he had no choice, as again, he searched his van for clothing. Finding a half decent pair of jeans, a blue shirt and an old jacket, Brett hit the road, carrying a small bag.

The term ' travelling light' was an apt description for Brett. Except for his shaving gear, the only other things he took with him, were his passport and a mixture of photos of his first wife Susan, and some happy snaps of Linda. Reaching the front gate, Brett sheepishly, looked towards the manager's office. He hoped to avoid any confrontation until he cleared his debt. It wasn't to be, as the manager seeing him coming, bolted out of his seat. Cursing loudly, he moved into Brett's path, in his hand he held a small baseball bat.

"Where are you going and where's my money you deadbeat!" He spat out, smacking the baseball bat into the palm of his left hand threateningly.

"I just got a cheque. I'm going to town to cash it." Brett answered, sidestepping around him, keeping away from that bat.

"You fucking lying piece of trash. You'd better come straight back with the money dipshit, I'll sell up your RV and everything you own." He chuckled, as Brett gave him the bird over his shoulder, and kept walking. "You stinking drunk, I'll crack your head wide open, if you do that again." He screamed, making Brett turn.

"Hey, you keep the RV, you deserve it. I'll keep the money I owe you." Brett smiled, blowing the surprised manager a kiss. Feeling free, he walked towards LA, leaving the manager cursing him, till he was out of hearing range.

The RV Park where he now used to live at was a good twenty miles from LA. With no other options, he decided to thumb a ride or walk if necessary. After twenty minutes of ambling along the roadside, an old truck overloaded with vegetables stopped. The driver looked like a typical dirt farmer of the area. Covered with grime, he wore an old faded pair of blue overalls. His most notable feature was his sunburnt face deeply lined with age.

Giving Brett a small smile of welcome, the farmer gestured for him to get in. Brett climbed in, thanking him for stopping. The farmer at first didn't talk much; so Brett settled back, listening to the radio.

"I judge you're leaving?" The farmer said as they neared LA. Brett was about to ask him how he knew when he saw his passport hanging out of his bag.

"Yeah, I've got a job offer, it's overseas."

"You sure do travel light." He replied showing a small grin.

"Yes, you could say I'm starting over." Brett smiled.

"You know this is the third time I've picked you up." This made Brett blink, as he tried to remember. "You wouldn't remember. Both times I brought you back here you were drunk as a monkey. The second time you vomited on my seat." He smiled. Brett, embarrassed, took several seconds to reply.

"I'm sorry there's no excuse for my behaviour. I'm an alcoholic." Brett realised that this was the first time he'd confessed to anyone, that he had a drinking problem. For some reason unknown to him, he then blurted out his whole life story, while the farmer just sat opposite, listening and driving. After twenty minutes, Brett finished his confession. Facing the window, looking out at the suburban sprawl, on the sly he wiped his eyes.

"You know the hardest part of being a drunk is admitting it, my friend? Maybe you've turned the corner?" The farmer told him.

"God I hope so and thanks for listening, and again, I'm sorry about throwing up in your truck," Brett said softly as they drove on.

Dropping him off in downtown LA, Brett thanked the farmer for the lift.

"Good luck young fella. I enjoyed this drive a lot better than the last two." The farmer chuckled softly, before driving off. Brett stood on the corner, watching the farmer till he turned down a side road. He felt for the first time, in a long time, optimistic about his future. Going straight to a bank, he cashed the cheque, after showing several different forms of identification, to a very suspicious bank clerk. 'Who could blame them', Brett smiled, seeing his reflection in a store window.

His next stop was a barber, getting a much-needed haircut. The next was a clothing store, where he purchased several suits and a variety of other clothing and footwear. Leaving his purchases, he walked down the street, buying some travel luggage, before returning. Putting on one of the suit's he'd purchased, he found the shop assistant, had kindly packed his other clothes in his new luggage. Thankful Brett gave him a good size tip, before hailing a cab.

Arriving at the Airport Hilton hotel, Brett booked into one of their best rooms, before ringing Qantas airlines to validate his ticket. Reserving a seat for a flight the following morning, he rang the number attached to the letter.

"Good afternoon Mr Heckle." A polite male voice answered.

"How did you know it was me?"

"This number was set up just for you Mr Heckle; I judge you're on your way?" Brett a bit apprehensive gave in, giving his flight number to the unknown polite man, before hanging up.

"Something isn't quite right here?" He murmured to himself, as he looked in the mirror opposite him. He saw the image of a confident man, on the way to the top again. "Well whatever happens to me, it's got to be better than getting evicted from that fucking RV Park." He assured himself chuckling.

Now came the hard part, as Brett hungry, went down to the restaurant. The desire to have just one drink made Brett shake, as everywhere he looked he saw people drinking. Ordering his food, he ate quickly, before leaving a good tip and retreating to his room. When booking the room, he'd asked for all alcohol to be removed, giving religious reasons. He was glad he had, as an outbreak of shaking possessed him, after he entered.

Taking a shower to cool down, Brett found after getting out, the urge to booze seemed to have withdrawn. Even his shaking had eased off. Taking it as a good sign, he turned in early, sleeping soundly.

The phone ringing the next morning woke him from a deep, peaceful sleep.

"Good morning Sir. You asked us to wake you at 8 sharp." The fresh dutiful voice informed him.

"Thanks very much." He answered sitting up. Stretching, feeling better than he'd felt in ages, he showered again, before dressing. Shaving, he looked at himself in the mirror seeing his bloodshot eyes had settled down losing their redness. Pride that he'd beaten back his inner demon gave him a sense of control, as packing his bags; he caught the lift down to the foyer.

Settling his account, giving the concierge a well done and a good tip for their trouble, he asked could he call a taxi for him. The concierge instead had the hotels limo drive him to the airport. It appeared the new Brett was making friends.

Arriving there, the chauffeur insisted on helping him carry his bags to the Qantas terminal. Giving him another good tip, Brett realised good service had its price, and while the money lasted, he thought he'd enjoy it. Walking to the desk, feeling upbeat, he showed his ticket to the cute girl behind the counter. She too was impressed with the well-dressed man. Seeing he held a first class ticket, she personally escorted him to the first class lounge.

On the way she engaged him in conversation wanting to know what business he was in. Giving little away, indicating it was to do with security; he felt her hip lightly brush against his as they walked along. She seemed more than impressed, wishing him a good flight and slipping her phone number to him, her eyes shining. Promising to ring her on his return, he settled in. 'God I could really get used to this treatment' he told himself as he was offered refreshments while he waited.

Sticking to soft drinks, eating little, he rested in the lounge leafing through a magazine while he waited. As time passed, he started to feel hungry. The lounge had a buffet style food service, so he helped himself to a small serving. Having been told by the over friendly counter girl, that the in-flight meals were superb, he decided to not overdo it. After finishing his meal, he was just about to return to his magazine, when a man in his early twenties sat down beside him, introducing himself as Andy.

He asked what was taking him to New Zealand. Brett was deliberately vague giving away very little, except he was there on business. Andy didn't seem to mind if his answers were guarded, suggesting places Brett could visit if he got time. Andy's wasn't a New Zealander, but Australian, something that wasn't surprising as the two countries were situated close together. Having never travelled to New Zealand or Australia, Brett took the time to listen to Andy's wealth of knowledge on the two places.

It occurred to him as he sat there listening, that he knew nothing about the two countries, but should. Something else he liked about Andy, he didn't drink, and at the moment that was a good thing.

Two hours of Andy happily chatting away, found them boarded their flight. Andy, he noticed, was sitting twenty rows behind him in Business class. Not that Brett would've minded him sitting with him, but it gave him a chance to just sit and plan for his interview. As the plane taxied down the runway, Brett looked out the window at his country, wondering if he would ever return, falling into another sound sleep.

A hand shaking him, brought him back to the flight, as a smiling hostess served him a spicy Italian pasta dinner. Returning the smile thanking her, he devoured the meal, surprised at how good it was. The hostess then returned, offering him a drink. Declining the alcohol, he settled on bottled water, before stretching his legs.

Walking towards the Business class section, he looked through to economy, seeing the people packed in like sardines. It occurred to him that it could've easily been him back there if his new, would be employer, had sent an ordinary ticket and not a first-class one.

"I'd still have taken it gladly" He admitted to himself, knowing this trip had pulled him from his life of despair, giving him another shot at living.

"What if you don't get the job?" A voice whispered to him, trying unsuccessfully to unsettle him.

"Then I'll find something else." He answered himself smiling.

Joining Andy at the bar, Brett grabbed a coke from the steward, before engaging Andy in conversation about their destination. Andy like before chatted on, his enthusiasm unstoppable, as several others joined them. A party atmosphere quickly developed as more and more first class and business class passengers joined them. Andy enjoying the limelight, failed to let the truth get in the way of his stories. These fictionists tales caused screams of laughter from the unbelieving, and in some cases intoxicated gathering.

It was one of the best flights Brett could remember. Even his honeymoon flight with Susan to Hawaii though enjoyable hadn't been anything like this he realised, enjoying the merriment. The eight-hour flight passed in no time as the cabin speaker softly as if embarrassed by ruining the moment, warned them they would be landing soon. Wishing each other a good time in New Zealand, the group reluctantly broke up, returning to their seats.

AUCKLAND AIRPORT

Passing through customs swiftly, with only a compulsory glance and stamp of his passport, Brett found himself in the arrival foyer, looking around for his lift. He saw Andy talking to a limo driver who held a sign with Brett's name on it. Walking over, Brett introduced himself to the driver. Benny, he found out knew Andy and was going to a friend's party later that night with him. He asked if it was okay if he tagged along, Brett happily agreed.

In the back of his mind, this coincidental meeting worried him, but he put it down to his excessive 'everyone's a bad guy' training at the FBI. The stretch limo was impressive as he and Andy piled in the back, while Benny drove. What surprised Brett was instead of heading to Auckland the Capital city, they headed towards the other side of the airport, following the fence line.

"What's going on Benny? I thought we'd be heading into town."

"You're flying somewhere else to meet your new employer," Benny answered as Andy remained quiet.

Brett looking at him realised he hadn't been fazed by the driver's answer. This he gathered meant he knew about this detour, something Brett thought they could've told him. A growing sense of unease spread over him, as the limo drove up beside a brilliant white coloured Gulfstream jet.

The plane itself didn't worry him, as he'd been on many flights on this type of aircraft in the FBI. Escorting prisoners or people being protected was common. What bothered him was the plane had no insignia on it, and no one was visible near it to greet him. He'd thought that after setting up a special phone line just for him, this would-be employer would have had someone here to meet him.

"End of the line Mr Heckle," Benny announced, as a quiet settled over the limo.

"Look, Benny, I'm not getting out of this car or on that plane until I know who's on it and where I'm going. Use your phone and have somebody tell me what's going on. Better still have them meet me here!" Brett announced as Andy beside him opened his door.

"You are getting on the plane Signor," Andy replied with a slight Spanish accent. At first, Brett wondered where he'd heard that voice before when it rocketed through his memory.

"You're that fucking Cuban hit man?" Brett exploded, preparing to leap at him.

"Don't be a fool Brett," Andy warned. From a small compartment on his door, Andy swiftly produced a small pistol. Pointing it directly at his stomach made Brett freeze. "At this distance, there is no way I'd miss. Get out Mr Heckle". Capitulating, Brett opened his door, as Andy quickly moved around to his side of the car to cover him. Signaling for Brett to go first, Andy, kept just out of reach, following. Behind him, Brett heard Andy tell the driver to go.

"You're an arsehole, Benny! When I get away from here, I'll find you and make you fucking eat that limo!" Brett shouted. The only response was a squeal of rubber, as Benny disappeared down the road, going home to count his pieces of silver, his betrayal completed. Calming down, Brett his mind in overdrive, tried to think of a way to turn the tables. 'Get him talking, maybe he'll drop his guard?' Brett thought to himself, as he approached the boarding ramp.

"So why bring me all the way out here Andy, if that's your name?" Brett asked as he walked up the short set of steps onto the plane.

"You'll know soon enough." He chuckled, as Brett entered the front compartment.

This section was set up with four rows of seats where the actual flight crew sat during take off. The next compartment, like on the FBI planes would be for the passengers to sit, followed by a conference, come lounge and dining area. He knew that each section of the plane was separated, by either bathroom or toilet areas. As he moved through the different sections, he hoped to find something to use as a weapon.

A fire extinguisher, a food tray, a paper, anything would do, but he needed it now. The chances were, once he entered the main cabin area, he'd soon be tied up, before some gruesome ritual killing. If he was going to get away, it had to be before he entered. 'They must be pretty pissed at the loss of all that money' He smiled, thinking back to the kidnapping. They'd taken his friend and held him in an attempt to gain a sizable amount of money.

They'd actually got the money, but the Treasury Department had tracked it to its source, seising it. 'Yeah, this is going to hurt' he concluded, as he came up empty at finding a weapon. To his front, a curtain blocked his view of what he took to be the central cabin area. Voices could be heard talking merrily from inside. Obviously they were waiting for him to entertain them with his slow agonizing death. Andy, if it was his name, followed several paces behind him, giving him little chance of grabbing his gun.

He was just about to part the curtain when an idea came to him. If he could grab one of his would-be abductors as he entered, he might be able to use them as a shield. Better still, they could be drinking, giving him a weapon in the shape of a glass. It wasn't much, but it was better than being gutted like a sacrificial goat. Pulling the curtain aside, he screamed loudly, before diving forward.

Catapulting into the surprised group, he grabbed a handful of hair, dragging a woman to her feet. Wrapping his hand around her throat, he backed up against a wall. He was just about to warn them to keep their distance when he looked towards the people. For several seconds he stood paralysed, trying to find the words.

"What the fuck is going on?"

ONE YEAR EARLIER

Adrian sat at his desk watching on his monitor, the next batch sample was being created. The lab area, where this sample was being genetically modified was in a sealed lab beside the workstation he was sitting in. Fear of contamination meant that no humans or outside air were allowed anywhere near the processing of Adrian's blights. Still, he had a bank of cameras watching it from every angle, to make sure that this one, unlike the previous ones, was perfect.

'Batch 68, will you be the one?' He smiled, looking at the clock on the wall. Each sample took just over 96 hours to grow to an effective size. This meant, as it was Wednesday, the blight wouldn't be ready till Monday at the earliest. This suited Adrian, as he was going to town on one of his 'get lucky hunting trips' night outs. Like usual, Brett would be going with him, giving him a little support with the opposite sex.

"Let's hope it works out for both of us?" Adrian said to himself, excited about his experiment and getting out. He'd waited all his life for this moment; he figured he might as well celebrate even though it was a little premature. Ringing Brett, he checked that tonight was still on. Getting a, 'bring a condom or two' answer in return, he heads home and showered. Promptly at 6, Brett picked him up driving towards the city.

"Where do you want to go?" Brett asked watching the road.

"I'm not sure. How about the bar Linda works in? It's got a good dance floor."

"Well Fred Astaire, we better hurry. I wouldn't want you to arrive late, the girls would be heartbroken?" Bret smirked, looking forward to the night out.

Sitting at the bar for over two hours, found Brett's mind becoming a fog of remorse. While Adrian wove his way around the dance floor trying to score, Brett imprisoned by his past remained sitting at the bar. Bored, deep in thought, he sat looking at his glass. Shaking his drink, he felt the ice tinkle against the sides. His life had become like that ice, he mused. Trapped, worthless, wasting away into nothingness, that was exactly how he felt.

Just a few years ago, he'd been on fire, a rising star. Now he was washed up, his achievements forgotten, as he fought just to stay afloat. Glancing down he noticed his left hand tremble slightly, as his craving fought to break free. 'Pull yourself together.' He chastised himself, as he stared into the mirror behind the bar. His reflection revealed a man just into his thirties.

To some, he was in his prime, to others he was peaking, on the way downhill. Still, wearing his sports jacket and trousers, with a casual blue shirt, with no tie, he still looked good. It was his eyes that revealed the truth. They looked tired, some would say worn out. Too many life-changing experiences and way too much booze he'd been told.

"Well, fuck them all" he snarled, his free hand clenching into a fist. Placing the glass forcefully on the bar, he swivelled around, facing the dance floor. What he saw was a gyrating mass of colour, as the emotionally charged dancers, pushed their bodies to the limit. Most couldn't dance to save their lives; others didn't have to, their scantily clad bodies making up for their lack of talent.

The dance he knew had nothing to do with rhythm; it was all about sex and getting some. Like the ancient tribal rituals, he'd seen on the Discovery channel, the people on the dance floor thrust and twisted everything they had, to ensnare a mate. Focusing on his reason for being here, Brett searched the crowd spotting Adrian. He was timidly talking to a full figured Brunette.

He guessed her age at around twenty-three, slightly older than Adrian and hundred years more experience. With a Californian regulation suntan and a tight-fitting white dress with a low cut front, she oozed sex. Adrian, he could see, was having trouble concentrating on her face, as he nervously pedalled his line.

"She's out of your league," Brett whispered smiling, watching the woman's body language. If she'd been interested in him, she would have leaned in, giving him an eye full. Instead, she'd crossed her legs creating a barrier between them, keeping him at a distance. Moreover, her eyes although watching him had taken on a bored look, darting glances past him towards the dance floor.

'Move on,' he felt like yelling, as the Brunette opened her bag and checked her mobile, before walking to the ladies room. Watching Adrian, he saw his shoulders droop, as he got the message. Unfazed by this setback, Adrian moved onto the dance floor, stalking his next victim. 'Poor kid couldn't get laid in a brothel,' Brett admitted, feeling for his assignment.

And that's precisely what Adrian was to him, an assignment nothing more. Professional babysitters, that's what Brett and the other members of the security detail were, himself a reject from the agency. Keep him safe and under surveillance, was what he'd been ordered to do and for over two years, it was all he'd done. It was his punishment, after his spectacular fall.

"Screw em all!" He said out loud, startling several patrons near him, as he turned back to the bar. Angry, losing focus, his eyes returned to his drink, as he felt the hunger twisting his guts. Coke and ice laughed back at him. He knew at that moment that he'd kill for a shot of Jack. Everywhere he looked he saw bourbon. People gulped it, sipped it, splashed it; he could almost taste it. Just the smell made his nose involuntarily inhale, as it tried to capture some of that magic.

As if coming out of a trance, Brett gazed towards the end of the bar, seeing Linda watching him.

"You've got no right to judge me!" He barked, turning back to the dance floor. He found Adrian on the dance floor, chatting up a skinny platinum blonde. She wasn't hard to look at either, as she rubbed herself up Adrian's left leg. 'Maybe he's got a chance this time' he thought smiling, trying to calm down.

"I wasn't judging you Brett" Linda's voice sounded from behind him, as he heard his glass being refilled with coke. Turning back towards her his anger fled.

"I know I'm sorry."

"I just worry about you, Brett. You look on the edge?'

"I'm okay Linda. Stop being concerned, I'm okay." Brett smiled.

"You want to come to my place after work, we could just talk?"

"I wish I could, but not tonight. I've got to keep an eye on Adrian. But thanks anyway." Brett lied, turning back to watch him.

"Okay. I just miss you," Linda whispered, moving away, serving another customer.

"You're a real arsehole Brett" He whispered to himself, watching the dance floor, not turning around.

Linda, like himself, was an alcoholic. She'd been a cop in Texas, and from what he'd heard a good one. She'd started out as a wet behind the ears rookie, working some of the meanest streets in the city. It was a hell of an introduction to the cops, but she'd done well, giving back a lot more than she took. On a late shift, Linda and her partner had been tailing a brand new Mercedes convertible. The guy had been swerving all over the road, yelling abuse at other drivers.

Hitting the lights and siren, the guy had flattened it, trying to evade being pulled over. They'd chased him for several miles until he sideswiped a truck, ending up in a ditch on the side of the road. Linda had dragged him kicking, out of the car. Smelling like a brewery, both officers knew he'd been drinking. While her partner checked out the driver's ID and registration, Linda read him his rights.

She then warned him he was going to be tested for driving under the influence. Seeing a pretty female cop, the clown had laid on the charm. Coming right up next to her, he'd told her how important his father was, suggesting he could help her career. Telling him to back off, she indicated the line on the side of the road, asking him to walk along it. Laughing, telling her 'no way', he instead, shoved his hand between her legs, asking if she liked it.

Waking up the next morning in the hospital with 3 stitches in his head and a broken wrist, Michael Battington, son of a local Senator yelled police brutality.

Even with her partner backing her up, she still got suspended for a month, pending a hearing into the incident. Michael Battington was granted bail for a surety of ten thousand dollars. His court case, if it got to court, was in six months time. Furious at her treatment, Linda stormed from the court going home. Once there reality stepped in. She had bills to pay and rent owing, the last thing she needed was a month without money.

The next day her boss dropped in for a coffee and a chat. Telling her she was a good cop and he wanted her back, he tried to convince her to drop the charges against Battington. He assured her that in exchange for her rolling over her suspension would be lifted. Staring at her Captain, she concluded that he'd been gotten to by the Senator. Swallowing her pride she agreed, knowing she had no choice.

A month after she dropped the charges, someone drove by her unit complex, throwing a brick through her window. It was followed by a phone call.

"How do you feel now pig? One night soon I'll be coming for you slut, be ready." Cruel laughter followed before the caller hung up.

The following weekend, found Michael Battington out with several of his friends at the opening of a nightclub. One of his father's business associates had invited him to the opening, to pay back his father for his help with the license. It was a sea of sex, drugs and booze until the cops arrived. Michael like everyone else was rounded up. This time he wouldn't be getting off so easily.

High as a kite, he was searched finding a couple of grams of cocaine in his pocket. This in itself wasn't a big deal to a young man with connections. Unfortunately, he took offence at being searched, hitting a cop knocking him down. Arrested and handcuffed the police angry, had given his car a going over.

Michael at this stage hadn't really been too worried. So he'd hit a cop and sniffed some dope, to a Senators son this was nothing. That changed, when they found a significant amount of cocaine in his car, he instantly sobered up, becoming worried.

"Hey, that's not mine. I'm being set up!" He screamed, as he was read his rights, and led towards a police van. Under the flash of the paparazzi cameras, Michael felt real shame and a little fear. 'How did the dope get in his car?' he asked himself mystified as to who would do it. As he was being thrown into the back of a van, he looked across the street to see someone waving. Focusing, he saw the smiling face of Linda.

Bail this time for the Senator's son was half a million. His plea of being setup fell on deaf ears this time. The judge having seen too many rich kids get off, made it known that if guilty, this criminal was going to jail. Despite his father's intervention, his court appearance was in just two weeks. Incensed at being set up, Michael, decided to pay Linda a visit at her home.

"I'll show her what a real man could do to a pig woman." He whispered as he left the police station.

Once home, he rang two of his friends, telling them what he planned. Excited, they arrived at his home that night preparing themselves. After a couple of hits and several drinks, they drove to her unit. Arriving at her front door dressed in black, wearing ski masks, they proceeded to break down the door.

The neighbourhood where Linda lived had a bad reputation, so like all the units in the complex; Linda's door was reinforced, giving her time to react. Running to the kitchen, she grabbed her pistol, kept hidden above the fridge. When the door finally caved in, the three would be rapist found Linda standing in the hallway facing them.

"Shit you weren't joking Michael, She's got Ho writing all over her." One of Michael's friends sniggered. It was only then that Linda realised she was standing in a pair of brief panties and a short tee shirt and nothing else.

"Put your hands above your heads, or I'll open fire." She warned, as the three cautiously moved towards her.

"You pull that trigger, and you're unemployed. You've seen what my old man can do." Michael threatened. Seeing her flinch at his words, Michael and his companions, moved forward. "And let's face it bitch, how many times would a pig woman, get to be screwed by someone famous." He sniggered, his friends joining in, as abandoning caution, the three surged forward laughing.

Their jovial mood ended abruptly, when Linda's automatic pistol erupted, belching lead. As the sound of gunfire echoed through the building, Michael's life came to an end, along with Linda's career.

Tossed out of the force, lucky not to go to jail, she turned to booze to cushion the fall. She soon ran out of friends, as her depression made them avoid her. Leaving Texas, she'd wandered through the US, ending up in LA. Here an old girlfriend found her and got her into AA, straightening her out. In the end, needing to make a living, she'd got a job in a bar, of all places. Brett had met her at an AA meeting when he first arrived in LA.

They hit it off, even having the occasional screw each other's brains out night at Brett's trailer. He knew she had feelings for him and wanted more, but his past unfinished business made that impossible. In the end, he just stayed away from her, hoping to cool things between them. Deep down he missed her, which was why when he came to town with Adrian; they always ended up at the bar where she worked.

Shaking himself, Brett returned his attention to Adrian. He was making some serious headway with the pretend blonde. She was all over him, grinding her sex against his thigh. Adrian gaining in confidence had pulled her into a tight embrace, showing her what he had. Giggling the girl pulled his head forward kissing him, thrusting her tongue into his mouth. Breaking the kiss, he whispered something in her ear getting a smile and a giggle in return.

His confidence on the rise, as well as everything else, he slid his hands down the waist of her dress grabbing two handfuls of her arse. The girl in return, lowered one of her hands, gripping him between his legs.

"By the look on his face, he'd be lucky to get off the dance floor without shooting his load," Brett said out loud, happy for him. Unfortunately, Adrian's wet dream was about to come to an abrupt end, as a sizeable muscled shadow loomed over him. The guy was a good forty pounds heavier and four inches taller than Adrian. He menacingly planted himself between the fading blonde and Adrian, sizing him up.

Stabbing him in the chest with his overgrown fingers, the giant started to talk and spit all over Adrian. Brett didn't have to read lips to see the guy was telling Adrian that he was going to turn him into dog meat. Springing to his feet, Brett ploughed his way through the crowd, coming up behind the new arrival. His plan was simple, stop Adrian's night and face from being ruined.

"Who said you could touch my girl?" The boyfriend shouted above the music, his bad breath making Adrian cringe, nearly as much as his size. His girlfriend in the meantime had been transformed from a tease to an angel, appearing innocent of trying to make Adrian prematurely satisfied.

"Why don't you take your girlfriend and piss off?" A voice suggested, from behind the Neanderthal boyfriend, making him spin towards the new threat.

"What are you his babysitter or something?" The boyfriend smiled, puffing himself up like a swamp toad.

"I'm his bodyguard friend. And unlike that sock you've got stuffed in the front of your pants, the bulge in my pants is a gun."

"You've got your own bodyguard?" The girlfriend practically purred, sensing money. This made her boyfriend turn towards her, thinking that maybe she'd been more than just a victim. Without another word he turned and led his fake blonde away, leaving Adrian as before without a woman.

"I thought she was the one?" Adrian smiled.

"Your pecker thinks anything with hair on it is the one." Brett retorted as they moved back towards the bar.

"Thanks for helping, she didn't mention a boyfriend."

"No problem, the guy was a bully, someone needed to shake him up."

"I didn't know you carried a gun when you take me out hunting?"

"I don't. But he didn't know that did he?" Brett smiled.

"Well, thanks anyway. We may as well go; I'm not exactly slaying them." Walking past the bar Brett nodded goodbye to Linda, as Adrian gave her a wave. Linda smiling, waved back to Adrian, her eyes though remained on Brett.

"She really likes you, doesn't she?" Adrian asked watching Brett's reaction. At first, he stopped, and Adrian thought he was going to explode. Instead, he started walking again.

"She's something special Adrian. She deserves better, let's leave it at that." Brett softly answered walking outside.

On their rare hunting trips to get Adrian laid, they'd used his allowance from the University to rent an apartment in LA. The plan was if Adrian scored, Brett would make himself scarce, leaving Adrian with his conquest in the apartment. Out of twenty plus trips to LA, Brett had only had to sleep elsewhere twice. One had worked out okay the other was a disaster.

The first was a young secretary, new in town, out for the first time with her girlfriends from work. She had country virgin written all over her, as she drank heavily with her girlfriends. She was trying to fit in, something always difficult for an innocent country girl. Brett watching realised her friends from work were setting her up. They were plying her with drinks, knowing she couldn't handle it. Women could be so bitchy, wanting the pretty new girl to make a fool of herself for their entertainment.

He guessed by the way they were watching the door that some male friend from their office would soon arrive. As part of their plan, he would offer his help, to take the poor girl supposedly home. Instead, he'd take her somewhere quiet and screw her arse off. Then the next day at work, he'd wait till the poor girl arrived, then boast about his conquest, destroying the poor girl's life. Thinking of having some fun of his own, Brett turned to Adrian.

Pointing the girl out, he told him he'd seen the girl watching him, suggesting he ask her for a dance. Seeing she was pretty, he readily agreed, sailing across the floor. Nervously in front of the other girls he asked her for a dance. Giggling she said yes, taking his hand they stumbled onto the floor.

Across the room, Brett watched the look of death the women gave Adrian. He was ruining their plans, as behind them a guy in a salesman suit appeared. Putting his arms around the waist of two of the women, he gave each a quick grope, smiling mischievously. Brett could see them discussing the developments, as the smile left the salesman's face, replaced for a split second by anger.

The smile returning, he walked out onto the dance floor putting his arms over the shoulders of Adrian and the virgin. Acting friendly he waved to the girls watching, smiling pleasantly. Brett was already moving, as the guy's friendly grip on Adrian became a vice, inflicting pain. It was crowded on the dance floor, no one noticed except the virgin. She at first thought the salesman was joking. Telling him to stop it, she watched as the salesman increased the pressure on Adrian.

Around them the dance went on, everyone oblivious to Adrian's pain. From out of the crowd, a kick smashed into the salesman's right leg crippling him. Crashing to the floor, the same foot kicked him in the face, breaking his nose and knocking him unconscious.

"Best you two leave." A voice told them from the crowd, as the women watching from the sideline; saw their male friend lying on the floor covered with blood. Adrian knew the voice, of course, so grabbing the girls arm he led her to the exit. Outside, Adrian walked her silently along the street to the bus stop; there she began to cry. Though still intoxicated, she knew her new friends had set her up.

She asked if Adrian would mind walking with her for a while. Adrian understanding happily agreed, placing his coat over her shoulders, as she explained what had occurred. Her name was Anita and against her parent's advice; she'd left home to find a job in the city. After a few dead-end interviews, she'd landed a job in an advertising firm.

Although the work was different to her job back home, her boss had advanced her because of her ability. The girls from the office who hadn't at first been happy with her advancement had asked her out. She thought they'd accepted her, now she knew the truth.

Adrian in turn, told her of him coming from Australia to study here, admitting he missed home and his friends. Together they continued to walk and talk getting to know each other, till feeling better Anita suggested they take a cab back to Adrian's hotel, for a drink. Hailing a cab, they sat together silently, till Anita taking the initiative, leaned across kissing him.

Arriving at the hotel, they had several drinks at the hotel's bar before Adrian suggested they go up to his room for a coffee. Once there the coffee was forgotten as Adrian led Anita to his bedroom. Giggling at their naivety, both took off their clothes in the dark. It became strangely quiet as naked they both climbed into the king size bed. For several minutes both of them lay timidly waiting for the other to take the initiative.

Hesitantly Adrian pulled Anita to him feeling her tense, as she felt his erection. Holding one of her hands he pulled it onto his member, letting her hold it. Kissing her, he felt her hand move back and forwards, as she experimented, her breathing coming faster as her excitement grew. Climbing on top of her Adrian spread her legs as Anita started to tremble.

Nervously she told him it was her first time, although he could feel her body pushing against him rubbing him. Promising to be gentle, Adrian put off the moment till he felt her legs spread wide apart, making his entry unavoidable.

Afterwards, they both laughed like small kids, secretly doing something naughty. When the laughter stopped, Anita climbed on top wanting this time to dominate. They'd spent the whole night, enjoying the passing of her virginity, two people, who hardly knew each other. To Anita, he would always be the one who saved her from her supposed friends.

Leaving early in the morning, feeling happy if not slightly embarrassed, she'd written down her number, giving it to him. Promising to ring her, he gave her a quick kiss goodbye. When he rang a few days later, he found she'd moved back home, leaving no way of contacting her. Although Adrian had been disappointed with her leaving, Brett quickly pointed out that he was looking at it the wrong way.

True she'd left, but he had scored a home run. This at least made Adrian a bit more confident, though he would've liked to have at least seen her again before she'd left. The second woman regrettably in seconds took his confidence and destroyed it.

She was hot, steaming hot. Right from the start, she'd singled Adrian out, and that should've warned Brett. In her late thirties, early forties, she had the confidence of a cougar. Poor Adrian didn't know what hit him, as she swayed to the music, her full firm body hypnotic. Brett too found he couldn't keep his eyes off her, as he also felt the man-eater's attraction. To top it off, she was an incredible dancer.

Every man in the place watched her, as she rubbed her body up against Adrian's. Sweating profusely, Adrian appeared drugged, as the woman wove her spell over him, enslaving him with her dance.

'Fuck is he in for a wild time' Brett thought doubts forgotten, as the cougar tired of the vertical foreplay, led Adrian to the door and outside.

In the taxi she'd teased Adrian to the point of no return, even the taxi driver had a hard-on. By the time they'd slid out of the cab, Adrian could hardly walk. Entering his apartment, she stripped off, walking naked to the bar getting them both a drink. Handing one to him, she took off his clothes kissing him and biting him playfully, driving him crazy. Reaching into her bag smiling evilly, she pulled out two pieces of rope. She told him she got off on tying up her lovers.

Adrian close to exploding excitedly agreed. As Adrian lay on the bed, she straddled him. Grabbing one arm at a time, she expertly tied each hand to the bedpost while Adrian obediently licked her nipples.

"Are you ready?" She asked rubbing her sex along his dick making him moan.

"You bet!" He screamed closing his eyes as she hovered above him, as her lips slowly slid down his chest, licking there way lower. Adrian, unable to bear the teasing any longer, ejaculated, screaming with both pleasure and frustration, as the cougar smiling, got off him. And that's how Brett found him the next day, humiliated and robbed, still tied up. She'd taken everything, his money, his credit cards and his clothing, leaving him humiliated, feeling a fool. Despite Brett's efforts to rebuild his confidence again, it had hurt him, leaving him wary.

That had been two months ago, and this was the first hunting trip since then. Brett had hoped it would have gone better. Adrian he realised, was no longer just an assignment, he had become a friend.

Adrian lay in his bed thinking about his life in LA and how different it was from his life at home. He knew if it wasn't for Brett and his project, he'd be long gone. When he first encountered Brett, he knew something was wrong. Behind his heavy drinking and tough guy stance, Adrian knew he was hurting. Lack of closure a psychologist would have pronounced. In simple terms, someone had killed his girlfriend and gotten away with it.

Their friendship hadn't started out as a perfect arrangement, Adrian though he liked him, was at first wary of him. Several times while accompanying him, Adrian had smelt alcohol on Brett's breath, once he'd had trouble driving. Although Adrian had remained silent, pretending not to notice, it had scared the shit out of him. Mystified by his drinking, Adrian had approached another ex-agent based at the University, asking about Brett's story. He had at first been reluctant to discuss Brett's past, in the end, knowing Adrian wanted to help him, he'd told him of Brett's career.

Four years ago, Brett was a rising star of the FBI's New York office. Intelligent, good looking and fit, he was a poster boy for the agency. Teaming up with Darren Crammer, an experienced field agent, they wove a path of mayhem through the drug cartels and organised crime families, which plagued New York. In one year alone, they seised over half a billion dollars in drugs and money, both receiving commendations from the President himself.

For a while, everyone thought the partnership between Crammer and Brett was the winning combination, until two years back things started to go wrong. On several raids, there'd been shootouts with the gangs. Several agents had been injured, with no drugs seized. An investigation into the raids had laid the blame on weak Intel and a Gung Ho attitude from mainly Brett.

He saw it differently, believing there was a mole in the office. Crammer didn't believe him, causing a split in their friendship. Inside the agency many thought Crammer had been a little jealous of Brett, letting him take the fall. Brett after being reprimanded and suspended for 10 weeks became obsessed with stopping the leak.

Keeping information on a coming raid to himself, he'd used the New York police force, instead of the FBI. Together they busted a major import operation, seizing three tons of heroin. It was the largest seisure of drugs in US history. Accolades flowed in from law enforcement groups throughout the country, but he lost the support of many in the FBI by going outside the agency.

A week after the drug bust, Brett along with his girlfriend Susan attended a medal ceremony hosted by the business community of New York. Twelve officers of the New York police department, plus Brett, received a medal and a special commendation, presented by the mayor personnel. It was an important night for Brett vindicating his belief that there was a mole. Susan who had reframed from drinking all evening nominated herself to drive home.

Brett noticed she'd been unusually silent during the night, so he asked her if there was a problem. Stopping she told him she was pregnant watching his response. Overjoyed by the news, he kissed her, suggesting they get married and look for a place to live away from the city. Relieved that he wanted the baby, she spent the rest of the trip planning where they'd move to. Susan bubbling with excitement, truly happy, turned into their street as it started to rain heavily.

Dropping Brett off at the front door rather than get wet, she continued around to the back entrance. The unit they lived in had underground parking at the rear. Usually, you'd use a key card to gain access, but it was being repaired. That was why Brett cut through the building to open the garage door at the rear from the inside. He was just pressing the button to open the rear door, when an avalanche of shots thundered against the door, making Brett dive to the ground.

With a sense of panic and impending doom, he waited for the roller door to slowly open. Through the pouring rain, he saw Susan's bullet-ridden body slumped over the steering wheel. Running to her hoping for a miracle, his face became a mask of pain, he'd checked her pulse. It was a waste of time, as she'd received several shots to the head and chest, she was gone. Brett his eyes glazed, pulled out his pistol and started down the alley, to where four men were entering a dark sedan.

In the downpour, the gunmen had opened fire, as soon as Brett's car stopped. They'd been hired to take care of the troublesome FBI agent who'd hurt a major drug cartel. They'd been given the agent's home address and his vehicles license plate. There'd been no mention of a girlfriend. Their only instruction was to make it bloody. Seeing his car was missing from his car parking spot, they'd check the apartment, finding it empty.

Concluding he was out somewhere they'd decided to wait in the alley and finish him as he stop to open the garage door. Even though it was raining heavily, they had no trouble identifying his car as it came to a stopped at the garage entrance. Seeing the blurred shape of one person outlined by the cars headlights, they opened fire.

The figure in the car having clearly received several shots to the head made the gunmen ceasefire.

Positive they'd silenced the agent permanently, they casually walked back to their vehicle. Getting into their car at the end of the block, they happily discussed what they'd do with their share of the money when the driver saw movement behind them. Shouting a warning, the driver reacting, started the car. Brett by this time had reached the vehicle, emptying his gun into it. The driver, being only superficially hurt, planted it. Roaring away he looked into the rearview mirror watching Brett frantically reloading.

"Shit!" The driver screamed throwing the car from side to side, as Brett took aim again. Firing another clip, he concentrated on the driver. Fatally hit, the driver lost control rolling the car over onto its roof. Walking calmly up to the overturned vehicle, Brett watched the surviving shooter try to crawl out of the back seat of the car. Placing his foot on the man's hand, stopping him, Brett applied pressure, asking his first question.

"Who sent you?" Receiving a groan and a fuck off instead, Brett gave him one more chance to tell him who'd hired them.

"You failed to kill me dirtbag, meaning your employer won't be happy, so for the last time, who sent you?"

"Who was in the car?" The shooter groaned, Brett eased off the pressure on his hand.

"The woman I was going to marry."

"Then this fuck up is your fault, for letting her go out with you pig." He laughed, "Now read me my rights."

"Not this time." Brett snarled, shooting him twice in the head. Making sure every one of them was dead, Brett returned to his car. Sitting down on the curb in the rain, he stared at Susan. "The arsehole was right it was my fault that you got killed!" He sobbed, cursing his stupidity, as he screamed out his rage. He was still there screaming, when the police arrived twenty minutes later.

Whoever paid for the contract killing was never found. The FBI investigation led by Crammer, found no proof of a mole. They concluded that Brett's lack of caution, had led the killers to his home. On stress leave at the time, Brett upon hearing the findings confronted Crammer. Blind with rage, he accused him in front of the whole office staff, of being the leak.

Crammer affronted by the accusation, shoved Brett away from him, telling him his carelessness had gotten his girlfriend killed. Brett, already over the edge and with several drinks on board, lost control. Screaming his rage, he savagely attacked Crammer. Pandemonium broke out as office staff witnessing the fight, shouted for help.

Four agents in the office at the time wrestled Brett to the ground. They held him there until the local police arrived and took him away. Charged with assault, he was indefinitely suspended, pending his dismissal from the FBI. With no one to turn to, Brett found solitude in a bottle.

The mayor hearing of his condition had interceded on his behalf, asking the head of the FBI to find him a job somewhere and get him help. Owing the mayor a favour, Brett's boss had thrown him a bone, assigning him to the University, as part of the Homeland security detail there. His employment there was unusual, as FBI usually didn't babysit students. They'd made an exception because of the sensitive government work being carried out there.

Brett knew he'd been dead-ended, but until his suspension ended, he was stuck here. His position there also had two conditions. One he would go to AA and stay away from the booze. The other was he kept away from

Crammer. Since being at the University, he'd fallen off the wagon several times, mostly while away from work. Only once had he been suspended. He'd turned up for work plastered.

His job that day was to escort Adrian to a seminar at a university two hours drive away. The Dean had just parked his car when Brett entered the car park nearly running him over. The Dean had gone ballistic; having two guards escort him off the property. When a different driver turned up to drive Adrian, he'd asked him where Brett was. Hearing he'd been suspended, Adrian had gone to the Dean.

Finding out they were going to fire him from the agency, as well as his job at the University, Adrian threatened to leave. Angry at being blackmailed, Dean Campbell reluctantly capitulated, winning one concession from Adrian. He insisted he didn't leave America until his work was completed. Adrian having no choice had agreed, as long as Brett never knew of this meeting. Since then he'd kept to the agreement, though he missed home.

"God I hope you were worth saving Brett," Adrian said aloud, thinking back to where it all began.

YOUNGER YEARS

Nerd, drip, four-eyes, geek, know it all and his favourite, freak. These were some of the many names, which Adrian had been taunted with during his time at High School. Born in America, Adrian's mum had moved to Australia after the death of his father. Home to Adrian now, was Northern New South Wales, the home of surfing, drugs and beautiful women. Adrian's claim to fame was not his surfing ability or his luck with the opposite sex. He was famous for his ability to grow plants.

From an early age, Adrian had worked with his mother Merle, on their small farm in the hinterland above Byron Bay. They grew Native plants for some of the country's leading retailers. Merle and her husband Andrew had been born in the USA. She worked at the Seven Mile Island nuclear power plant as an electronics engineer, while Andrew was a leading research scientist, working at a local University. His field was applied science, and many computer systems ran on his patented software. The spill at the nuclear plant made them both rethink their priorities.

Andrew for a while before the accident had been unhappy with Merle working at the plant. Adrian was now four and was being babysat at home, while they both worked. Both parents thought they were missing out on being with him. After the leak, he decided it was time to sell his patents and move away. With the money, he hoped to buy some land and take it easy with Merle, raising Adrian between them. He decided after informing his wife, he'd give his notice, working till the end of the year.

Telling Merle of his plans that night, he was surprised when she burst into tears. She'd been at the time waiting to tell him she was again pregnant and wanted to stay home and raise the two children. Over the moon with happiness at having a second child, Andrew decided to not wait but resign and give the University two weeks notice.

The next morning Merle walked Andrew to his car promising a special night when he came home. Excited Merle planned a special meal to celebrate. At four Andrew rang telling her he'd had a fight with the Dean over the right to sell his patents. He explained to her, how the Dean had asked him to wait for the full board to convene that night to discuss it.

Confident he'd win the argument, he promised to ring her after the meeting and before he drove home. It was the last time she would talk to him.

When he didn't come home by twelve, Merle rang the University. Getting a 'we know nothing' response, she rang the police. They found his car an hour later, upside down in a ditch. It appeared someone had forced him off the road and kept going. Merle in shock was rushed to the hospital, she lost her baby. Several weeks passed before feeling recovered enough, she went to the police with her suspicions. She told them about his fight with the Dean, and how he'd promised to ring her after his meeting with the University board before driving home.

The police dutifully went to the University and confronted the Dean. Dean Jeffries told them no one at the University knew anything about a board meeting or Andrew's patents. The police at first were suspicious, but without anything to go on, they reluctantly dropped the investigation. Merle heartbroken found her job at the power plant suddenly terminated with no explanation. With little money to spare, she engaged a small town detective to find out what was going on.

Four days after he started investigating, he was run down by a hit and run driver. Again the police investigated before dropping the case with no suspects. The Dean in answer to Merle's accusations threatened her with legal action. He denied that the patents were ever in Andrew's name, producing copies of a contract between Andrew and themselves giving all rights to the University. Finding discrepancies with Andrew's signature, Merle knowing she was being lied too, decided to continue the fight in court.

Coming home after talking to a lawyer, Merle found her babysitter bound and gagged. Horrified she swiftly untied her babysitter who fled. With growing apprehension, she then approached Adrian's room. To her great relief and surprise, she found him sleeping soundly unaware of what had occurred. A note attached to his cot warned her to leave town. Collapsing onto the floor, Merle spent the night gripped by fear, sobbing at her near loss of her only son.

The next day she packed what she could carry and left. Moving to Australia, she started a new life with her son, changing their family name back to her maiden name of Hayes. The only bright spot for Merle in all this was Andrew, had a significant life assurance policy. This helped her buy a small property in the Byron hinterland, where she started their small nursery.

Running a nursery hadn't been easy for his mother. Growing plants was a hard competitive business to be in, especially being new to the country and starting an alternative nursery. She became part of a group that had turned their backs on herbicides and insecticides, producing a clean, environmentally friendly product. This put them at an extreme financial disadvantage, as the major nurseries could produce thousands of plants with reduced labour cost by spraying.

Not being able to afford labour, Adrian at the age of ten, started to help out at his mum's nursery. He was given the tedious job of weeding the plants and checking them for insect damage. His mother was surprised, when not only did his plants grow; they had minimal damage from insects. She found he had cross-planted different species which discouraged weed growth and at the same time prevented insect damage.

He did this by natural means, something even the experts had trouble with. By the age of fourteen, he was taking an active part in running the farm. He designed new plant layout, grafting different species to prevent insect damage and encouraging growth. The once-struggling nursery now employed 10 workers allowing his mother to take it easy and enjoy life.

Trying to simplify programs for the workers, Adrian wrote a small book, laying out instructions on his planting methods. It wasn't long before other nurseries in the area seeing Merle's nurseries success, asked for copies. The only thing that bugged him during this time was that he hadn't been able to completely eradicate weeds. With his mother's business secure, Adrian focused on his own career and his fixation with weeds.

He had an insatiable hunger for knowledge spending hours studying plant growth and later cell regeneration. His gift for horticulture carried him through high school, where all the cool kids spent most of their time at the beach. Mr Invisible he was nicknamed by one girl in his class because he always had his nose in a book.

In a way, this was true, as he used his books to shield him from what was going on around him. Though his studies filled his waking hours, he wasn't as indifferent to the opposite sex as his classmates thought. One girl, in particular, had always drawn his attention. Kim was his height, slim and attractive, the type of girl whose smile melted a young man's heart. She'd been born in Japan where her Australian father met her Japanese mother.

They'd moved back to Byron to further their careers and get Kim an Aussie education. Like him, she was quiet and brilliant. Her exam marks put her well above the other students, and she would've easily topped the class, except for him. It wasn't until the last year of school that he'd worked up the courage to ask her out. It had been a major disaster, she'd laughed in his face.

"Go out with a nerd, you've got to be kidding!" She screamed out, mainly for the benefit of the students. The classroom had exploded with laughter crushing him, breaking his heart for all to see. The high school had been hard on Kim as well. By rejecting Adrian, she saw the chance to leave the nerd label she had behind. In a way it worked, elevating her into the cool section of the students, unfortunately, it left Adrian isolated and alone.

Humiliated, Adrian from then on, concentrated on his work. He gave women a wide berth, afraid of being hurt again. Kim knew she'd wronged him and tried to several times to repair their friendship. Regrettably, it was too late, the damage had been done. From then on, he kept his distance. A month later, his life changed dramatically.

As part of his entry exam to University, he was asked to write his thesis on weed control. He'd written a paper on genetic plant growth and the future of manipulating plant DNA to control weeds. The research was groundbreaking, changing the way many scientists looked at plant growth. Scholarships to Universities all over the world rained down on him.

The local newspapers getting wind of it printed his thesis, with a picture of Adrian. They then tried to explain what it meant to the public. Girls, who before had laughed at him, suddenly found a celebrity sitting next to them in class. Several girls in his class openly flirted with him, one actually slept with him, much to his amazement and nearly instant gratification.

Their attention although appreciated and greatly enjoyed, came too late. Two weeks after his thesis appeared in the paper, he was summoned to the Principal's office. There he was introduced to Milton Cambell, the Dean of a Think-tank University in California. The university was devoted to gathering the best minds in the world, to solve the world's most pressing problems. Dean Campbell radiated confidence, explaining to Adrian the inner workings of his campus.

The Dean oozed charm. In his early forties, well dressed with a vibrant go get-um attitude, Campbell professionally laid out his Universities advantages. Promising Adrian access to equipment and facilities far superior to any other University in the world, the Dean knew he had Adrian hooked. The scholarship came with a healthy allowance and travel to and from Australia at least four times a year.

To Adrian it was a chance to prove his theories and reach his full potential, he readily accepted. His mother didn't share his blind faith in people that they didn't know. She had first-hand experiences of dealing with corporate America. Merle was not happy wanting assurances. She demanded a guarantee that he'd be safe and free to leave if he wished to. There was also the question of his research while there. The Dean, in the end, had several prominent Australians ring Adrian's mother.

They guaranteed his safety while there, and his interest would be protected, which sealed the deal. Adrian ecstatic hugged his mother thanking her. Hugging him back smiling, she hid her misgivings at him going.

"Don't worry mum, I've got it all worked out." He assured her as if reading her mind.

"Your father said the same thing, Adrian." She answered distantly, remembering the last day she saw him. Seeing the look on Adrian's face, she brightened up putting it behind her. "You better get going if you're going to meet your friends?" She reminded him, changing the subject.

"Will you be okay?" He asked concerned.

"I'll be okay, get going and don't drink too much." She smiled. Watching him hurry off, she thought again of Andrew, wondering if maybe she should tell Adrian, what truly happened to his father.

Only having two weeks left before his departure, Brett grabbed a lift with one of the farm workers to Byron Bay. Adrian could count his good friends on the one hand and he knew most would be at the local hotel overlooking Byron beach today. It wasn't that they drank at the pub all the time. It was an arrangement they had made since leaving school, to meet the second Friday of each month, until they left for University or work.

Of course, they all knew about the University in America's offer. So it was no surprise to them when Adrian practically ran into the pub. Spotting them in the corner, he waved madly to them, hurrying over.

"He's either going to the American, or he's got lucky again?" Robbo chuckled to the others, as Adrian crashed into a vacant chair beside him. Robbo was one of Adrian's closest friends. He didn't go to school with him; he worked at his mum's nursery.

He'd turned up about three years ago aged fifteen and needing a job. Adrian's mum at first thought he should be in school. When she checked, she found out that he'd been expelled, having discipline problems. Ringing his home to check, Robbo's mum had told her that her husband had split. This left her with four children to raise on her own. Short of money, Robbo, being the eldest, took it upon himself, to find work.

Feeling for his predicament, she reluctantly agreed to give him a go, although she worried about his attitude after being expelled. He proved to be a hard worker and good at what he did. Adrian at first had trouble talking to him. While he thought of complex solutions to solve long-term problems, Robbo being practical, went with what worked.

It was as if Adrian was talking Chinese and Robbo was speaking Italian, they had nothing in common. Argument followed argument as both pushed their ideas. Adrian's mum, in the end, became the referee, judging each problem on merits. Sometimes Adrian won, sometimes he didn't. This went on for over six months, until the fire.

Some idiot camping in the foothills had decided to light a small fire to cook his lunch, during the summer heat. The bush was tinder dry, and his small fire became an inferno. Sweeping down from the hills it engulfed everything in its path. With a hot easterly wind from the inland deserts pushing it, the flames roared down the hillsides heading straight for their nursery.

At the time Adrian's mum was away in Sydney leaving just him and three other workers at the farm. Two were working with him in the packing shed; Robbo was out in one of the back blocks clearing scrub, for a new planting. The workers took one look at the flames coming and fled, yelling for him to come with them. Adrian, who was also fifteen at the time, knew they all had only minutes to get away before the only road was blocked.

Telling them to go, he ran to the farm Ute, driving out to towards where Robbo was working. Looking in the rearview mirror, he saw the flames cross the road behind the fleeing workers.

"Well, at least they made it," Adrian said out loud, putting a cushion under him so he could see clearly out the windscreen.The smoke became so thick he had trouble following the track, let alone breathing. Continuing to search, he slowed down honking the horn continuously, trying to alert Robbo to his presence. The only return sound he heard was the roar of the fire. Scared, thinking he'd made the wrong decision in staying, he saw a blur of movement to his right.

Stopping, praying it was Robbo, he saw him staggering out of the burning scrub, stumbling towards him. With his shirt over his mouth, his legs and arms exposed to the flames, Robbo ran blindly towards the honking horn. Ripping the side door open, he jumped in gasping for breath. Looking at his puffed up eyes full of cinders and his burnt arms and legs; Adrian was amazed he'd made it.

"Thanks." Robbo croaked out, as he gulped down some lukewarm water, left in a jerry can in case the Ute's radiator boiled over. Adrian coughing wet a piece of rag covering his mouth replying with a nod. The surrounding area was a sea of flames, as Adrian seeking an escape route, turned the Ute downhill driving towards the valley below.

He knew that this side of the property bordered a river, giving him a glimmer of hope. The heat outside the vehicle was now beyond what a person could stand. Robbo having cleared the cinders from his eyes upended the water container over both of them, as the engine gave out. Dodging yet another tree, Adrian tried to weave his way through the light scrub knowing to stop was to die.

Both men knew there was no road or track to follow, the only thing keeping the vehicle going, was its downhill momentum. Twice they cannoned into large trees unable to avoid them, as the vehicle mortally wounded, staggered on, the heat inside continued to grow. Spotting the river through the smoke, Adrian spun the wheel turning towards it.

The fire now encircled the vehicle, shutting off their vision completely. Both young men close to passing out looked at each other, nodding their understanding of the situation. Adrian fearing the end closed his eyes, thinking of his life, his mum and his unknown dad. A bone-jarring screech of metal sounding beneath them, made him reopen them. The vehicle had hit a large rock propelling them into the air.

Thrown against the roof, Adrian hung onto the steering wheel as with a sudden thud, the Ute nosedived into the river. From being burnt alive the two men now faced drowning, as the Ute started to submerge. Trying the doors, they found they were both blocked, as the water rose rapidly to their necks. In panic, they both kicked out wildly, trying desperately to break the windscreen. Tired from excessive heat exhaustion, neither had the strength to break the glass; in the end, giving up, they waited their fate.

Amazingly that's as deep as the water got, as the vehicle hit bottom in the middle of the river. Around them, flames leapt into the air, crossing the river. Once across, they surged forward, consuming everything in its path. Inside the Ute, buried in the river the two young men remained safe. Neither knew how long they sat there, until looking at each other they burst into laughter, celebrating their escape.

With clearer heads, they used a crowbar kept under the seat, to lever the windscreen out. Freeing themselves, they swam to the shoreline, where they rested. Sitting in the shallows, they pondered their next move when the noise of a helicopter thudded its way up the river. Shouting, waving their arms, they watched it pause above them. Coming into land on the riverbank beside them, they walked together to it, smiling like they'd won the lottery.

From that day forward they were somehow joined together as brothers, always there for each other.

"It's the first. I'm going to America!" Adrian answered them excitedly.

"We will miss you," Dan replied, from across the table as Michael agreeing went to the bar for drinks. Both Dan and Michael had become friends with Adrian in high school. All four friends shared a love of horticulture, although Robbo was the only one employed in the field. Adrian had never been sure that Robbo liked the other two, but they were Adrian's mates, and that was enough.

"I'll miss you," Robbo said looking at the floor, hiding his emotion.

"I'll keep in touch and anyway someone's got to look after my mum, you know what she's like."

"Let's face it, she like me better than you anyway."
Robbo laughed, the others joining in. Dan seemed about
to say something but hesitated.

"Is there something you want to say Dan?" Adrian
asked.

"It's just you're going overseas to study and change
the world, but have you ever heard of anyone connected
with agriculture making serious money? Let's face it,
none of us are exactly chick magnets. I figured at least if
you had money, you'd get laid."

"Don't count me in that group. I don't need money."
Robbo sniggered.

"I hate to agree with Dan, but he's right Adrian. These
Universities prey on clever kids. You usually end up with
nothing." Michael added.

"Well I'll have to surprise you al then by coming back
filthy rich," Adrian smiled, the others chuckling at his
optimism.

Sipping their beers, the group of friends, settled in,
watching the parade of scantily clad girls walking by.
They were an odd group, three being skinny nerds, while
Robbo was tall, tanned and all muscle. He got the eye
from a lot of the passing trade, while the others
pretending the looks were for them.

"Kim was here earlier looking for you," Robbo said
softly, for Adrian's ears only.

"I'm not sure why?

"She likes you, Adrian. A blind man can see that."

"Well, she's got a funny way of showing it."

"Hey, it's been a long time since she had a go at you.
Be a man and forgive her." Robbo said raising his voice,
as the other two looked over, wondering what was going
on. Adrian was about to bite back when it occurred to him

that this was the first time Robbo had pushed him to do anything. Sitting there his anger fled.

"You're right.' Was all he said, as Robbo reached across grabbing him in a headlock, laughing.

"What the fuck are you two doing?" Dan exclaimed, trying to look cool, while two of his friends wrestled like children. Adrian was just about to answer, when looking up he saw Kim with three of her friends standing over them.

"Is there room for us?" Kim smiled. Dan and Michael open mouthed exploded from their seats, fetching chairs and making room. As the girls sat down a quiet settled over the table, as Robbo starting sniggering at the instant state of nerves his friend had developed.

"What are you celebrating?" Kim asked looking at Adrian.

"I'm going overseas to University. I leave in two weeks." Kim's friends congratulated him, while Kim staring at him got up and ran towards the beach. Everyone froze wondering what was going on.

"Go after her Adrian! We'll take really good care of her friends." Robbo promised, as Dan and Michael opposite, went red at his disguised suggestion. This made Robbo burst into laughter.

Adrian heard none of this, his whole attention on Kim. Without a word, he jumped to his feet, following her. Behind him, Robbo happy in a festive mood downed his beer, before turning back to his companions.

"So girls, what are we going to do while they're gone?"

Adrian found Kim sitting on a swing crying. At first, he wasn't sure what to do, in the end, he sat down on the swing next to hers.

"I'm so sorry Adrian. I've missed being your friend." She whispered.

"I'm sorry to Kim. I should've let it go a long time ago."

"And now you're going. I wanted so much to spend some time with you, now it's too late." Getting up she put out her hand for him to hold, leading him down onto the beach. They walked hand in hand along the beach, south towards the headlands. Here lay a small inlet, watched over by a lighthouse high above it on a rugged escarpment. They didn't talk; they just walked, enjoying the sun's heat on their bodies.

"Let's go for a swim?" Kim suggested. Moving above the high tide mark on the sand they stripped off their clothing. Adrian luckily had worn his Speedos under his shorts that day, as he hadn't really planned to go swimming. Kim, on the other hand, had been down the beach all day. Under her shorts and top, she wore a pale blue bikini. She had grown from a skinny teenage girl to a full figured woman. He found his eyes drawn to her bikini, which strained to keep her large breasts in check.

As much as her body enticed him, his gaze shifted to her face. Her Japanese heritage gave her an ageless beauty. Her dark brown eyes seemed to be looking right through him. Reaching across he pulled her to him, kissing her. Her lips were soft, and at the same time firm, pushing back against his. He'd kissed girls before, especially Helen, who'd slept with him, but this was something different. It was as if somehow he sensed the kiss had changed him.

Breaking away from him, Kim giggled before pushing him backwards and running towards the water. Caught momentarily off balance, Adrian recovering chased her. Gaining steadily on her, he tackled her as they both crashed into an oncoming wave both going under.

Breaking the surface spluttering, Adrian saw Kim attempting to swim away. Surging through the water, he leapt forward, catching hold of her legs as she screamed playfully.

Pulling her to him, he kissed her again holding her tightly. This time she didn't break away; instead, she wrapped her legs around his waist pulling him into a tight embrace. Adrian never wanted that kiss to end, even in the cold ocean water, he knew he wanted to make love to her. Breaking away from him, having felt his hunger growing, Kim looked down between them smiling.

"I'm not Helen Adrian. I want more than a one night stand." She said softly, before pulling him close and biting him playfully on the ear. Adrian wasn't sure what to say, when a huge wave crashed into them, pushing them both under. Breaking the surface sputtering, Adrian found Kim watching for him, before turning and swimming towards the beach.

Following her, he came up beside her, watching her dry herself. Finished, she passed her towel to him. Adrian still wasn't sure what to say. He was both surprised and frustrated by her. He sensed Kim wasn't impressed with him sleeping with Helen but why? It wasn't as if they were a couple or anything at the time. Maybe she like him was aware that there was something unique between them?

"I've never felt like this before Kim," Adrian confessed as he stood watching her dress. It was a simple statement, straight from his heart. Kim stopped dressing. She knew looking at him, that he meant it. Taking his hand, she kissed it.

"We have 14 days. Let's not waste them." She said softly, as finishing dressing, they walked back towards the hotel.

Arriving back they found Dan and Michael sitting dejectedly. Robbo had taken two of the girls and left. Both had tried for the remaining girl, but she'd decided on an early night, going.

"That Robbo's a greedy pig." Dan slurred out. He was slightly drunk and smarting over missing out on a girl.

"So what are we going to do tonight?" Michael asked, wanting to move on.

"Sorry, but Adrian's taking me home." Kim smiled, leading him outside.

"That's just great." Dan moaned, totally disillusioned.

"Think of it this way. Two of us got lucky." Michael pointed out smiling.

"Oh for fuck sake shut up!" Dan groaned, walking to the bar, hoping to drown his sorrows.

After they had left poor Dan and Michael at the hotel, Kim and Adrian wandered through Byron shopping centre, enjoying the afternoon, which quickly changed to night. Getting something to eat, Kim invited him back to her place to meet her parents. This was a problem, because Kim lived south of Byron, in a small seaside village. Adrian knew there was no public transport there.

"That would be great, but I'd have to ring my mum and see if she can pick me up."

"I've got my own car, Adrian. My parents bought it for me, knowing I'd need it to drive to University. That's if I manage to get in of course."

"What are you studying?"

"Law like my father, it seems to be a barrister runs in my blood." She giggled.

"Where?"

"In Sydney, I'd say. My father's sister lives there, I'm going to stay with her."

"You would be good at anything you did." Adrian admitted, squeezing her hand as they walked to her car. It was a small VW beetle, not an ancient one, though it wasn't new either. It had a convertible top, which she admitted rarely using, fearing it wouldn't go back up. It was funny her driving Adrian mused, as they headed south. He had never got around to getting his license, always being too busy. Now with a girl he wanted to see living some distance away, he realised he'd been stupid for not thinking of it.

Arriving at the village, they travelled south of the town, driving up onto the coastal plateau above it. Here the houses dominated the coastline, giving uninterrupted views of the coast. He didn't have to ask how her family was doing, as they drove up a private driveway stopping in front of a four-car garage. In was an impressive house. Adrian silently wished he'd worn better clothes than his shorts, Hawaiian shirt and thongs.

To his relief, Kim's father met them at the door dressed the same way. It appeared he dressed as he liked, when not at the office. Adrian received a warm welcome. Both her parents had read the article about him and his thesis, even understanding it, to a point. Evidently they considered him as a good potential boyfriend for Kim.

After a polite grilling by her parents on what he was doing and where he was going, Adrian was relieved he wasn't up against Kim's father in court. They seemed particularly interested in the Think-tank University he was going to.

"Watch yourself there Adrian. Most of those Universities expect a large percentage of anything you invent or patent. Remember that when you sign anything." He warned.

"My mum said the same thing. On the other hand, it's the ideal situation I'm looking for. There I can attempt my experiment. I can't see any alternatve."

"Well if you have doubts, run it past Kim or me, she's just as clever." Her father smiled clearly proud of her. After talking till 8 in the night, Adrian noticed while he and Kim watched TV, both parents carrying bags down to the garage.

"Are you going somewhere?" Adrian asked.

"We're going to Sydney to overseer a lawsuit. Kim's offered to drop us and then take you home." He informed him, hurrying to check his luggage.

"You don't mind do you?" Kim asked.

"Of course I don't. It will allow me to spend more time with you." He smiled.

Instead of VW, Kim drove her father's Mercedes under strict instructions to watch her speed. Time being short, they dropped her parents at the drop-off point, Kim saying her farewells while Adrian carried their bags inside. After waving goodbye, Kim again got behind the wheel driving away. Even though it would take longer, Kim told him she'd take her father's car home first. There she'd swap it for hers, not wanting anything to happen to it.

Back at her family's house, Kim suggested he sleepover. This would save her driving back home on her own in the dark. She was also forceful, in pointing out that he'd be staying in the guestroom. Agreeing, he rang his mum while she had a shower. Getting a 'what's going on' okay from her, he rang Robbo for some advice. By the sound of it he was having quite a night, as the two girls constantly cut into the conversation.

Surrendering the bedroom to them, he moved into the lounge room so they could talk. He first asked for a full report on what happened. Adrian told him everything, leaving nothing out. Robbo remained silent while he told him everything, listening to every detail, till he'd finished.

"Do you care for her?" Robbo asked. Adrian stood there thinking about his friend's question. Sure he'd only been with Kim for a short time, but he felt there was something special going on between them.

"Yes I do, what do you think?" Adrian, after his pause, finally answered.

"Look it's your first serious date Adrian, and you don't want to do something stupid. I'd suggest letting her make the first move. If she doesn't, well you've got nearly two weeks before you leave, best not ruin it."

"What like taking two girls home would ruin it?" Adrian replied.

"This isn't the same Adrian you know that. You're serious about her, while I'm just having fun." Thanking him for his advice, Adrian moved to the TV room waiting.

Freshly showered, Kim sat down beside him, wearing silk pyjamas. The pants were long right to her feet, and the top had sleeves covering her arms. To Adrian, it made no difference. With her hair wet hanging loosely in a thick bundle down the side of her neck, she looked alluring. Neither said anything, as they both leaned towards each other kissing.

Adrian had no idea how long they kissed; it was the best evening of his life. No words were exchanged just the constant moan or groan as they sought each other trying to get ever closer. In the end, Kim broke away. She had a slight sheen to her body. Her pyjamas were damp from sweating, and her breathing was ragged as if she'd run a mile.

"It's time for bed Adrian, I must go now." She whispered as if betraying them both by leaving. Standing, she showed him to the guestroom, where they kissed again until she pushed him away. "I've got to go." She confessed dancing away. Smiling back at him, she left him standing there, happy beyond belief and at same time miserable. Closing the door, Adrian walked to the enormous bed feeling its emptiness, wondering if he should go to her.

"Don't ruin it," He told himself, taking off his clothes. With no pyjamas, he slept naked trying not to think of Kim and the arousal she'd caused. Unable to sleep, he stared at the ceiling powerless as vision after vision of her swamped his mind. In the end, sleep came upon him, although his dreams were still filled with her.

They spent the next day together as well. Arriving at his home with Kim, Merle insisted she stay for dinner. Adrian's mother was surprised at a young woman coming home with him. He'd never showed much interest in the opposite sex, now suddenly when he was about to travel overseas, in walked a beautiful young woman. Merle could see he was besotted with her, as she was with him, making her wonder what was going on.

Kim stayed the night at his home, sitting up with Adrian's mum, while Adrian checked the nursery. Merle confessed her fears to Kim, about Adrian going back to America. She told her how she had secretly checked out the University where he was going. It was run by the same group, which had run the Campus where Adrian's father had worked.

Reassuring her, Kim pointing out how what happened to Adrian's dad could've been just an accident. Privately she was wary. The next morning Kim left, thinking of what Merle had said.

"You know Adrian, your mums worried about you," Kim confessed as she drove back towards Byron.

"I know," Adrian replied running his hand up her thigh, making her slap his hand smiling.

"I'm serious."

"I know, It's just I have this all worked out, trust me." Adrian smiled his hand again on her thigh. This time she didn't slap it away.

They spent the rest of the day at the beach before driving back to Kim parent's house. She was expecting them to be home. Instead she found a message on the phone apologising, but they were held up in court and would be home tomorrow night.

"Do you mind staying in the guest room another night?"

"No that would be great," Adrian answered happily to be just with her. Ringing his mum telling her the situation, she gave him the 'you're going overseas soon' talk, warning him to be careful. Promising to be home early the next day, he waited for Kim's return. Instead of returning in her pyjamas, she arrived in her bikini.

"How about a swim?" She suggested, throwing him a pair of her father's board shorts. Changing he met her outside at the pool. It was just getting dark, as Adrian arrived at the pool. She was already in swimming, although in a large pebbled coated pool she seemed more a shadowy shape just visible. Sitting down, dangling his feet into the pool Adrian watched her glide through the water.

As he placed his hands on the poolside to steady himself before hopping in, his hands came to rest on material. Picking it up, he realised it was a piece of Kim's bikini.

'She is naked' His brain screamed, as he froze on the side of the pool instead of jumping in. Coming towards him, she rested her arms on the side of the pool, looking up at him. Bending forward he kissed her. He tried to look her straight in the eyes, trying to pretend he was okay with a naked woman. Holding her, still kissing her, his hands ran down her back feeling nothing but smooth skin. Giving up, his eyes wandered down her face to her breast, hidden just below the water's surface.

"Hold me, Adrian. I want to be with you tonight." She whispered, as Adrian lower himself into the water next to her. The water was freezing, cooling his problem, as they held each other, kissing fervently, hungrily devouring each other's uncertainties. Pulling her up out of the water he towelled her body, then her hair, while all the time struggling with each other to get closer. Wiping himself, dropping his board shorts onto the ground, he picked her up carrying her inside.

Taking her to the guest room where he'd slept before, he lowered her onto the bed climbing on top of her. Kim screamed in both pain and pleasure when he took her virginity. The pain was over quickly, as moaning with pleasure, she spent her first night with a man as a woman. Every fantasy, everything he'd dreamt of doing with her the last time he'd slept here, came true that night. There were no boundaries between them as they explored each other's bodies, satisfying their every question until in the end, they slept.

Waking early, they again made love again going swimming. Kim parents not coming home the next night allowed him to stay another night. Adrian again rang his mother promising to be home the next morning for sure. He knew that his mum was fully aware of what he was doing, but she didn't judge him, something he was thankful for. That night Adrian told Kim all his goals in life and what he wanted to achieve in America. She at first was silent not wanting to cast doubts on his life plan. In the end, she agreed to help him, knowing he wouldn't be swayed from his goal, and she loved him.

Over the days that remained, Adrian became less interested in going overseas wanting to delay it. Kim not wanting to be the reason for stopping his plans, told him to go. Assuring him she'd keep in touch, she arranged to meet him in Sydney on his first break from Uni. In the end, he knew he had to go, promising to return as quickly as he could.

Sitting on the plane watching his country fade into the distance Adrian kept thinking of Kim. What was she to him he asked himself? He felt something deep for her as if she'd become part of him. Helen would always be the first girl he bedded, but for some reason, Kim seemed to be the one he wanted. The way they felt about each other he realised, was what made the difference. While Helen had been a mind-blowing experience, Kim's lovemaking had been intense, all-consuming. He wasn't sure if he loved her, but he wanted her, which made it pretty close.

"It would have to wait." He told himself. Putting emotions aside, he started calculating his future work, wondering how long it would take his plan to bear fruit.

CALIFORNIA

Arriving at Los Angeles Airport, Adrian was overwhelmed by the organised chaos that surrounded him. Patiently he waited in a never-ending queue at customs, watching the ever moving parade of people. Most pushed past him in the line, he gathered they either didn't see him or just didn't care. Some looked back at him realising they'd pushed in front, though no one gave up their spot. Reaching the desk he handed over his passport to the Customs officer, who silently perused his customs statement.

"What is your reason for visiting the United States?" The Customs guard asked in a bored tone.

"I'm here to study at University Sir. I'm studying" was all he got out.

"Next," The officer shouted, practically throwing his passport back to him, indicating for him to move on. Nodding his thanks, Adrian gathered up his papers moving towards the baggage pick up area. Wondering what he'd gotten himself into, Adrian grabbed his bags off the carousel, walking towards the exit doors. Feeling depressed, missing his friends, Adrian tried to locate his lift to the Uni. Not sure which way he was going, he sat down on a bench.

"Hello, are you Adrian? My name is Emma." A voice sang in his ears, as looking up he saw a woman of about twenty-five smiling down at him. To say she was attractive didn't do her justice. She was tall just over six feet, with long tanned legs, slightly concealed by a tight fitting black skirt. This was accentuated by a white silk blouse, which failed to hide her ample cleavage. If this wasn't enough, she had a movie-star looking face with deep penetrating blue eyes. Stammering out a 'Yes, that's my name,' Adrian slowly stood up, following her outside.

Walking behind her was quite a treat, as Adrian watched the outline of her underwear rhythmically bounce from side to side. Outside she approached a limousine, where a dutiful driver, opened the side door for them. Climbing in after her he couldn't keep his eyes off her legs as her skirt rode up her thighs, smiling she pulled it down getting comfortable. His bags were at some stage taken from him by the chauffeur, when he wasn't sure, being practically hypnotised by Emma's body.

Sitting opposite him, Adrian felt her legs brush against his supposedly by accident, teasing him, her eyes sparkling, watching him. She then told him about the campus, filling him in on what went on. In between staring at her body and listening, Adrian got a rough idea of the layout of where he'd be spending the next three years, thanking God he'd come.

Arriving at the front gates Adrian moved his gaze from Emma to the two security guards checking their ID's. Emma seeing his attention focus on the guards instead of her, jumped in.

"The security here at the gate is for our student's protection. Once through this gate you'll find security is minimal." She assured him, seeing his eyes refocus on her, meaning he believed her.

Driving to the main admin building, Emma led the way inside, while his luggage was taken to his unit. Here he was taken to Dean Campbell's office where he greeted him. After a quick rundown on how things worked the Dean pulled out a contract for Adrian to sign. He explained it was the usual arrangement between a student studying and the University covering cost through a percentage of any patents he recorded while working here.

In other words, they took a chunk of anything he invented. Knowing without their backing he'd achieve nothing, he quickly signed. Emma watching him sign looked at the Dean, her trademark smile creasing her lips. The Dean too looked pleased, as pressing a button on his desk he summoned an underling. After a handshake with the Dean and a small peck on the cheek from Emma, one of the Dean's assistants showed Adrian to his unit.

It was located across from his lab and office workspace in a high-security section of the campus. To say the least, it was impressive. With sweeping views of the mountains the one bedroom unit contained everything a young man could ask for, 'except one thing,' he smiled.

After a quick shower and seeing the sun starting to go down, Adrian decided to look around the University grounds before getting something to eat.

Walking for an hour built up Adrian's appetite. Following the signs, he strolled towards the cafeteria. It was packed and Adrian found himself in a long line. The wait was worth it though, as the food was first class. Sitting at one of the many tables he swapped small talk with other students, several of them young women. Though some were attractive he didn't seem to get anywhere with them, even with his Aussie accent.

Feeling tired, he decided to turn in, walking back to his unit. Outside waiting on the walkway, stood a man of about thirty, in a well tailored sports jacket and pants. He wasn't wearing a tie, having the front two buttons of his shirt unbuttoned. It gave him a relaxed, businessman type look.

Seeing Adrian approaching, he slipped something into his pocket before introducing himself. Brett Heckle was his name. He informed him, that he was part of the campus security. His job was to watch over students especially when they left the campus. As he explained many students, like Adrian, were working on special assignments that corporate companies may try to obtain, by any means.

As a precaution, when Adrian or any other students decided on an outing, a security agent would tag along, just in case. Personally, Adrian thought it was over the top, but the guy seemed sincere even though the smell of bourbon wafted from him as he talked. Walking back to his room with him Brett asked if there was anything special he needed.

"Emma's phone number would be nice." Adrian smiled, making Brett laugh.

"She'd eat you alive." He replied, before realising what he said, causing both of them to laugh. Promising instead to take him to LA when he had earned a break, Brett left still chuckling. Inside his room, Adrian considered what Brett had offered. It would be good to go out with another male as company in search of the opposite sex. He still considered Kim special to him, but he was here alone and needed some type of escape from his studies.

THE PROJECT

As the Dean had promised Adrian found the labs well equipped with the latest in research equipment. He immediately started work, using the campus' computer system to record his progress. What he was attempting was, to say the least extraordinary. Since only minor research had been carried out on DNA plant mapping, he would first have to gather multiple samples of plant life.

From weeds to vegetables from fungi to trees, the more extensive the genetic sample, the more information he could gather on each species, the better. Finding the actual growth cells in each plant was his goal. With it, he could then target one specific area of the plant. While working at the nursery back home, he had a great many encounters with an insidious plant killer called Phytophthora. It attacked plants by infecting the root system, strangling growth.

Adrian had isolated the genetic code that gave the disease its ability to attack its host. By manipulating this cell, he believed he could tailor it to eliminate a specific growth, without affecting the surrounding plant life.

On the bright side, many scientists over the years had studied the DNA on a wide range of plant groups for other reasons. By gathering this data on these plants, he could cut down on time required if he'd started from scratch. That aside he would first have to design a software program to gather the information, then analyse it, following his tight perimeters.

After three months he'd barely touched the surface. His program was at least finished. Going to the Dean, he asked if he could have a separate computer system for his DNA data collecting software. The Dean he found for security reasons was against having a stand-alone system. Instead, he had the software uploaded to the University's secure network.

In some ways, it was a pain, as security clearance was needed to gain access. On the other hand, the network guaranteed his data was secured, something he liked. Finished, for the moment, he decided on a break, flying back to Australia.

Landing first in Sydney, he arranged to spend a couple of days there with Kim. After several passionate kisses, she swiftly loaded him into her VW. As she drove along, she told him what she'd been up to. She was doing well at Uni, settling in at her auntie's home. Travelling there, Kim introduced him to her auntie who made dinner while they caught up.

One thing Adrian had brought with him was his copy of the University's contract that he'd signed. After dinner in her room, he gave it to her, asking if she could check it. A transformation came over her, as she took the contract turning each page slowly reading it in detail. It was a side of her he hadn't seen since High school, as she absorbed the information of each page, working it over in her mind.

Two hours of studying the documents and Kim looked over at Adrian to find him asleep. Shaking him, smiling at his lack of interest, she placed the contract on the coffee table.

"It is the vaguest document I've ever read." She pronounced, sounding none too happy. "It could mean you get nothing for your research or everything. The actual breakdown depends completely on the University's discretion.

"So it's okay then?"

"No it's not Adrian. They own you and it's not just while you're at Uni. Any future developments even after you leave Uni belong to them as well. There's something else too, I did some checking with some friends at other American Universities'. That Think-tank you're going to has some powerful friends. Most people who study there end up with hardly any income, their patents end up in the University's name." She told him.

"They deceived me too." Adrian murmured, Kim, noticed he had an unreadable expression on his face.

"Don't worry. Here in Australia you can take them to court and win. In America, I'm afraid you can't do anything."

"Well, mum was right. Makes you wonder about what happened to dad. Anyway, once I'm finished my research, then I'll worry about it. And anyway I'm a clever man I'll stick to my plan." Adrian smiled, forgetting work and concentrating on Kim. Walking to her door, he locked it, returning to her.

"I was wondering if you still wanted me." Kim giggled, as she slowly, teasingly, stripped.

After spending three days with Kim, Adrian travelled home checking on his mother and catching up with Robbo. Adrian found he'd enrolled in the local University, doing distance education from home. He was studying Spanish as well as Agriculture, something Adrian had suggested. Aside from furthering his education, he hadn't changed, enjoying working on the farm and chasing women. Adrian's finding his time was over, flew back to America and his research.

It took the whole of the first year to collect and load the DNA of the significant percentage of plant life on Earth onto his program. This in itself was a significant achievement, as he watched his program grow and expand. Self-educating itself as it went, Adrian knew it would take the software some time to find the key. Looking for the key growth cell was like looking for a needle in a whole countryside of hay, not just a bale.

Another year passed and still the program sifted through the data looking for the key. Up till now, Adrian had travelled home frequently visiting Kim and his family. It was at this stage that he'd saved Brett's job, meaning anymore trip back home would have to wait. At least he could talk with Kim and his family spending many hours a week on the phone catching up.

Two years two months and two days from the day he arrived on the campus, Adrian walked into his lab to see the computer sitting idle. It had found what Adrian had been waiting for. The Dean hearing the news immediately arranged for a secure section of the University nursery complex to be put at his disposal.

It was a dangerous time. All experiments had to be rigorously contained in the blocks allowed for them. Each one was sealed, having its own secure air system. This was to stop the accidental release of his DNA viruses or blights as Adrian called them, out into the surrounding area. At the start, some had no effects at all, while others killed everything. Andy the head gardener strictly controlled all experiments in the nursery. After each test of Adrian's blights, Andy would incinerate the entire block, to avoid the risk of the viruses spreading.

Andy watched Adrian work with a growing sense of unease. The kid was clever, maybe the most gifted DNA manipulator he'd seen. The problem was, he couldn't see the danger his research could be used for. He was so fixed on wiping out weeds he couldn't see the ramifications of his gene research. The Dean, on the other hand, was well aware of consequences.

On one of his many visits lately, he had asked Andy what he thought about the project. At first, Andy was reluctant to reply, knowing the Dean's reputation for a bad temper. In the end, concerned about the outcome, he spoke up.

"We're playing with fire Milton. I myself think his research is beyond what we can achieve at the moment, with our level of technology."

"Adrian is confident he can achieve it."

"Then God help us all. No one should have the power that blight will deliver to its owner." Andy told him; clearly thinking Adrian would not be the owner.

"Just do your job, Andy. Let me worry about control." Milton answered distantly, walking away. Andy watched him leave, seeing the look of self-imposed destiny lighting his face.

"I shouldn't have mentioned God." Andy murmured to himself, seeing the thirst for power it had caused in the Dean.

THE BREAKTHROUGH

"Out of bed lover boy, it's time to go back to work," Brett ordered, dragging Adrian's blankets off him. Adrian yawning shook himself, before swiftly dressing. Brett was surprised by his speed. He was usually slow in getting going, especially after a night out.

"Why so fired up?"

"I start field testing a new strain of my blight this week. I'm pretty confident that this could be the one." Adrian answered excitedly.

"Still cutting me in for a tenth?"

"That was the deal." Adrian smiled. On his first trip out hunting with Brett, he had jokingly asked Brett for his fee for showing him around. He'd replied he'd take ten percent after the University took their share. Brett had laughed, knowing that Adrian had figured out he'd been shafted by the Uni.

"Honestly Adrian you know you could bargain with them if you think you're close."

"I've thought about it. The problem is I'm not sure exactly what the cut is, I might be worried about nothing."

"Still, I would ask beforehand, your bargaining position would be stronger." Brett knew he couldn't push it. If Milton found out he'd been advising Adrian, he'd be fire on the spot.

"I've always wondered Brett, why the agency sends men here to work the security details. Isn't that usually done by private firms?"

"Yeah it's strange, but I gather the research here is cutting edge. Obviously, someone high up thinks it's worth our involvement. On the other hand, it could be a place you dump burnt out agents."

"Maybe it's both?" Adrian replied, fending off one of his shoes, thrown by Brett.

The drive back was mostly silent as both men thought about their lives. Brett felt guilty over Linda, promising he'd ring her once he knocked off. Adrian pondered asking the Dean about the percentage. He was happy with his progress his plan was in full swing. Maybe he should be asking about his share.

Once back, Brett dropped Adrian at his unit complex, where he changed and hurried down to the lab. Checking the latest batch number 67 he saw another failure. Deciding to go to the nursery he started out by picking up a snack from the cafeteria. Eating as he walked, he arrived at the nursery to find Andy incinerating his latest blight. Seeing it was pointless staying, he thought again, of Brett's advice, as he strolled back to his lab.

"I may as well get it over with." He said out loud, as changing direction he walked to the admin building. Asking to see the Dean, he waited.

Dean Campbell watched Adrian on a monitor on his desk; he could see he looked agitated. Emma was also in his office going over assessments of each of their more promising students work.

"What do you think he's here for?"

"He looks nervous, so I'd say it's about something to do with his contract," Emma answered.

"How do you know it's not about his experiment?"

"I watched him work. He's in complete control of his project, there's no nervousness there. No, it's got to be something about us to make him so fidgety. There's also the report from Brett the other day, where he asked about his percentage." Emma smiled.

"You're right, I forgot about that. He must be getting close to a breakthrough, or he wouldn't be here." He smiled back. "How do you think we should handle it?"

"Let me take care of him. He's off balance when near me."

"Okay, I'll use the back door. You can promise him anything; just don't put it in writing." The Dean smiled leaving.

Once the Dean had departed, Emma undid two buttons on her blouse, before applying some light touches to her makeup. Checking her appearance, she then pressed the intercom, asking the secretary to have him come in. Watching the monitor, she saw him take a few breaths calming down. He then marched in.

"Adrian, how are you? The Dean's had to leave on business, can I help?"

"I was going to ask him about the contract I'd sign. It was unclear on the percentage I got from my work." Adrian squeaked out, his eyes drawn to her cleavage.

"Don't you trust us?"

"It's not that, it's just it would be nice to know what I get out of all this research."

"You know Adrian it's expensive to run a facility like this, with the huge amount of equipment and expertise we supply. You can understand that your research though important, have relatively little commercial applications."

"I think you could be wrong there. I worked in my parent's nursery; weed control is a huge expense. Once my research is finished, it could revolutionise the industry." He pointed out.

"Yes, you're right. The problem is, once your method is used if it works, there's no need to use it again. That means there isn't any return business." Adrian sat there staring at her breasts unable to think of anything else to say. "Look how about I talk to the Dean, and I'll come over one night to your unit, and we'll discuss it further." She smiled, resting her hand lightly on his thigh. Adrian overcome by her proximity and her captivating perfume, readily agreed.

Leaving the admin office, Adrian thought more of Emma's visit than the research. Going to the lab, he carefully opened the airtight sealed area where his latest blight sample was stored. Checking everything was in order, he applied the batch number to his latest DNA hybrid. Batch 68 the label read, as he sealed it into an unbreakable container.

"Let's go 68, we've waited long enough." He said confidently sealing the lab. Walking across to the nursery Adrian could feel everything coming together. Handing Andy the cylinder, Adrian stared at the block provided. It was a mixture of corn, wheat and maize with interlaced rows of weeds. The weed blocks contained a pest common to many parts of the world called Cabana grass. It grew like sugarcane and was hard to remove once it established itself.

"This will be a good test," Adrian said confidently.

"Batch 68, that's quite a few tries isn't it?" Andy pointed out.

"I've got a good feeling about this one Andy."

"Funny, I've got the opposite about it." Andy muttered as he checked the room making sure it was airtight. Taking the sample, he placed it in a sealed time-release capsule. It was timed to let them exit the block, at which time the capsule would open, deploying the blight.

"How'd you go with Adrian?" Milton asked entering his room to see Emma still working there.

"I was right; he was worried about his percentage. I said I'd discuss it with you, and then go over it again with him at his unit. It seemed to placate him" she smiled.

"Good keep him happy for now, later it won't matter." He chuckled. "Now if you could excuse me I've got some work to do." He continued dismissing her. Emma surprised, left with an acknowledging smile, inside she was worried. Lately, Milton had become distant from her, not confiding in her like he used to. She made a note to find out why.

The next morning at 0530 Andy on time checked the plant room of the Complex. All systems were running normally, though the sprinkler system appeared to have turned on at 0300. This was unusual as it was programmed for 0500. Recording the fault, knowing this didn't affect any experiments in progress, he moved out into the complex checking each block. Making notes of each blocks progress, he came to Adrian's.

Almost immediately he saw the dark rows where the Cabana grass had been planted. It was completely dead the entire planting.

"Holly shit!" He cursed, as a feeling of impending doom settled over him. Moving to the other rows, he found no sign of any problem. Mystified and at the same time scared, Andy stood staring at the dead row of weeds.

"My God. What do I do now?" He said out loud, sitting down, taking in the kill. 'You could incinerate it all and pretend it had been over ineffective, targeting all the plantings' he told himself. He considered that such a result could put the kid's research back years, if not halt it completely. Then again another country could be working on the same project at this very moment, and his interference could jeopardise his country's advantage.

After several minutes of quiet contemplation on what to do, he started collecting samples and correlating his data. Andy finished, went to the shower block, vigorously scrubbing before changing. Next, dreading it, he telephoned Dean Campbell, telling him what had occurred.

"I hope we all don't live to regret this." He mumbled to himself, as he waited for the arrival of the man who would be king.

Twenty minutes after the call, the Dean arrived with several of his security men, including Brett. Cordoning off the nursery area, Brett accompanied the Dean inside.

Brett observed that Andy seemed worried by the results, while Dean Campbell looked like he would wet himself, his excitement evident.

"My God, he did it! I can't believe he got it be so effective, so quickly." Milton spluttered out excitedly.

"I think we should incinerate the whole block immediately," Andy suggested.

"I think you're overreacting Andy."

"I don't think so, Milton. This is the first test of Blight No 68, we have no way of knowing if it can mutate into a wholesale killer of all plants."

"Okay, for now, we'll just keep it locked down." The Dean said before stopping. "Actually open all the adjoining blocks, Andy. Let's give it two weeks, and then we can see if it does only affect the targeted species."

"That's actually a good idea Milton. You may ruin countless experiments by other students, but on the other hand, it could be a good test. There are at least 280 different species of plants in the nurseries at the moment. If in say three weeks there is no change in their health, we'll know the target plant was indeed the only effected species. On the other hand, if other plants start to be affected, we can incinerate the entire complex and contain it." Andy grudgingly admitted.

"Okay, we'll give it three weeks instead of two to be absolutely sure. For now, no one but you goes in or out. The only exception is Adrian, as he will probably want to see the result and carry out further tests. Brett will oversee security here until the complex is cleared." Milton told them, moving towards the entry. "And both of you, don't talk to anyone, am I understood?" Both Brett and Andy nodded their understanding, as Milton waved for Brett to come with him.

Brett dutifully walked beside the Dean thinking. He'd remained silent during the exchange between Andy and the Dean, slowly piecing together what was going on. Adrian he suspected had made a blight, which attacked certain, specified plants. He knew from Adrian he was researching a way to eradicate weeds, he must have found it.

If that were so, why was Andy so worried by the development? The fact the Dean was stationing guards here, meant some people weren't going to be happy.

"Dean, what's this discovery all about and how much security are we going to need?"

"Adrian's just opened Pandora's box." Seeing Brett didn't understand he explained. "He's opened the door to a major discovery. This will make America great again." Milton exclaimed, his whole face lighting up. "As for security, it might be needed here indefinitely and beefed up, maybe doubled. This project will be kept as secret as possible Brett and keep Adrian under guard, no leaving the campus for any reason. Put at least two men on him at all times." Milton stressed.

"He mightn't be too happy about that Milton, and he isn't an American citizen."

"I don't give a shit what he is or what he wants. I'll have him declared a security risk if need be. Just do as you're told, I'll worry about any fallout." The Dean spat out leaving.

Once away from Brett the Dean picked up his phone calling his office. His excitement at Adrian's discovery was overwhelming at first, now he had two problems. The first was he was sick and tired of Andy's overcautious stand on everything to do with the nursery. Wanting three weeks to test, when the blight had worked overnight was ridiculous. He was getting old; it was time to retire him.

The other problem was Brett; he was too involved with Adrian for his own good.

Telling his secretary to get the paperwork rolling to terminate both of them, he decided to wait for three weeks. It would be better that way to send them both packing, just when they thought they'd be sharing the glory of Adrian's success. He could just imagine their faces when he had them both marched off the property. Feeling on a high again he walked briskly to his office to spread the news to the right people.

Brett at the nursery door, stood deep in thought watching Milton go. He had suppressed the urge to flatten the smartarse; knowing getting fired wouldn't help the situation. How he wondered would this breakthrough make America great again? The Dean was really revved up, meaning something big was about to occur. How would killing weeds do that? He was just about to brief his guards of their duties when Andy appeared beside him.

"I suppose he's off to tell the board of the latest cash cow," Andy grumbled. Brett could see he wanted to get something off his chest.

"It can't be bad for the world to get rid of some weeds," Brett answered baiting him.

"That's the problem with you Brett, you think small. This DNA sequencing can be programmed to attack anything. From forest to food crops, nothing is safe. Look at Iran or North Korea, how long would they hold out if we destroyed their food crops? And remember how the President promised he'd deal with the drug cartels. I'd say illegal drugs crops will be the first to go, as a warning to our country's enemies." Andy looking at Brett, suddenly realised he'd said too much. "I've got to go

Brett. Let's keep this between us. He said softly, wanting a response.

"Forget it Andy I won't mention it to anyone," Brett assured him, as Andy nodding his thanks walked away. Brett recognised that Andy was scared of either the discovery or being found to have talked about it.

"An end to the drug trade, is it even possible?" Brett asked himself, as he checked the building's security. Sure you could hurt them badly, but there were synthetic drugs that could be used to fill the gap. Still, it would change control of the market, from large cartels to nickel and dime traders. There was going to be a lot of people more than a little upset by this discovery. Brett decided he'd double-checked the security system, before assigning more men to the nursery. Leaving after making sure everything was okay Brett pondered how safe Adrian would be here.

Dean Campbell's confidence in Adrian's success was overpowering. Not waiting the three weeks, till the blight was proven safe, he contacted the board members, informing them of Adrian's progress and what it meant. He suggested a board meeting to discuss how they should handle the discovery. Next, he contacted Home Security, asking for additional men.

The request was met with a less than enthusiastic response. Homeland security, of course, wanted to know why he needed such a massive increase in manpower. Telling them the project was top secret didn't cut it with them. In the end, they agreed to have someone sent out to evaluate the project's merits. Milton far from happy decided to wait until the Board meeting. He was sure that once the board became aware of the blights capability, pressure could be applied to the right people. Smiling he thought again of the applications of this blight and the percentage of patent he would receive.

"You look like you're having a special day." Emma smiled, entering his office.

"The kid pulled it off! I can't believe he did it."

"Is it that big a deal?"

"Emma, it will rival Microsoft."

"What about Adrian's share, he's bound to bring it up now it's proven." She asked, surprised by Milton's optimism.

"I don't see a problem. Even one percent could be worth at least a hundred million. I'm sure the board won't care."

"Well, I'll go over tonight and soften him up. Who knows what else he might come up with if he's kept happy?"

"I don't care what you promise him, we can always deny it, just keep him here. Screw his brains out if you have to, I don't care what you do, as long as he stays put." Emma speechless at what he was asking, nodded her understanding, leaving.

Milton watched Emma leave, a small smile sitting snugly on his lips.

"She needs this job. She'll do what she's told to, or I'll find someone who will." He chuckled feeling invincible, as he happily started preparing for his board meeting.

Walking back to her office Emma upset thought about Milton's treatment of her. To him now she was just an intelligent hooker. She'd been surprised by his smug confidence, that she would whore for him just to keep Adrian happy. Now alone it occurred to her that maybe she should consider her future. When she'd first started here as Milton's assistant, she knew her job included keeping the male students happy.

At her first interview, Milton had laid it out that he expected her to go the extra yard for him. She'd stripped off there and then, letting him do what he liked. To say the least, she got the job, although from then on Milton had kept his distance, separating business from pleasure. Lately, she'd noticed him taking an interest in a young secretary who'd just started in administration.

"He's grooming her to take my place." She spat out; knowing her employment here was limited by her looks. Emma knew she was still beautiful, but she wasn't getting any younger. "Maybe it was time to consider getting married, maybe to a rich scientist," she smiled. True Adrian was younger than her by a few years, but in the office yesterday he couldn't keep his eyes off her.

As second in command here, she had a good salary, but not nearly enough to get by on, if she was replaced. With the money, Adrian would be receiving she could live the rest of her life in luxury, and all she had to do was keep him happy. One night with her and she knew he'd be ensnared for the rest of his life. The more she thought about it, the better the idea sounded.

"Just one night!" She giggled, "And I do look gorgeous in white!"

When Adrian approached the nursery complex, no one had to tell him something had happened. Guards patrolled the building, and the front doors were locked tight, two things usually not necessary at a nursery. After showing his ID, he proceeded to the test area, finding Andy there, studying the Cabana grass.

"It worked?" Adrian asked excitedly.

"Yes, it did Adrian. To tell you the truth, I didn't think it was possible."

"What testing sequence will you follow now to make sure it only targets desired species?"

"We've already started. The Dean had all the adjacent blocks opened. There are over 180 species, being grown at the moment here, which is a good cross-section of the plant world."

"I can't wait to try it outside in the real world Andy. Can you imagine the difference having weeds free crops will have on our farmers?"

"Look, Adrian, you're a bright kid, but think of the other uses your blight could be used for."

"I don't understand, what do you mean?"

"Anything can be targeted, Adrian. Did you ever think they might use your discovery as a weapon?" Adrian stared at Andy as if he'd awoken from a coma.

"I never thought of that. Surely my discovery will be tightly controlled?"

"I'm sure it will be. Maybe I shouldn't have said anything." Silence settled over the two men, as Brett approached from behind them.

"What's the problem?" Brett asked, sensing by the silence that something was wrong.

"Nothing, we were discussing the testing process for future deployments." Andy volunteered moving away. Adrian continued to stand there as if working something out in his head.

"You're starting to worry me, kid. What's wrong?"

"Andy thought I was naive, that my research might be being used for other purposes." Looking at Brett, he saw him hesitate. "It's true isn't it?"

"Yes I think the owners of the University intend to use it to benefit the country and at the same time become quite wealthy." Turning, looking crestfallen, Adrian walked out of the nursery complex towards his lab. Brett watched him go feeling somehow he'd betrayed him. Picking his phone up, he called the security office.

"What's up Brett?" Brenan in charge of security answered.

"Could be nothing, but my assignment Adrian just found out his research mightn't be used as he thought it would. Can you make sure he can't delete his research?" Brett asked.

"Sure thing, we'll put a hold on his ability to delete files."

"Thanks might be nothing, though it's best to be sure," Brett told him hanging up. Standing in the doorway, he watched Adrian enter his lab, feeling again that he'd betrayed him.

PARTNERS

When Dean Campbell rang his partners, he was immediately told to get on a plane to Washington. A little surprised by their reaction, he did as he was told, booking a flight. Arriving at the airport, the Dean was approached by two men, in business suits. Identifying themselves as Homeland Security, they steered him towards a private jet waiting on the tarmac.

"What's going on?" He asked as he was led through a metal detector.

"You'll know soon enough." He was told, as a pretty brunette flight stewardess led him to his seat. Moments later Senator Jonathon Jeffries one of his business partners, seated himself beside him.

"Senator, do you know what's going on?"

"Sorry we have to tell you this way Milton, but you only have two partners, me and the Government. The other ten board members of your University are just people we hired to look the part. We thought it best to keep it low key that the Government was sponsoring research through a University Think-tank." The Senator waited while Milton chewed over what he said.

"Then do I still receive a percentage of the patents?"

"Of course you do. The business side of the University is still the same. Unfortunately, this breakthrough is a bit beyond profit. This is a National Security issue. You'll still get your bonus, just in an around about way."

"Okay I can understand you would want to keep that secret, but why am I here?"

"The President's been briefed on this project. Since it has National ramifications, we thought we'd get your input on the breakthrough at a meeting we're holding in Washington today."

"I can see no problem, other than I have no notes?" The Dean replied apprehensively.

"We just want you to explain simply what this research means. I'm sure the President will be grateful." The Senator smiled, as their plane taxied, taking off. Milton stared out the window, watching the plane gain altitude as he dreamed of his blossoming career. The Senator, seated several rows back, studying him. "He's greedy as,' he smiled knowingly. "Makes it that much easier to play him,' He chuckled, thinking of the money this blight would make him, not the Government.

Arriving at Washington, the Senator's limousine rushed them to the Pentagon. Security was a formality for the Senator. Milton on the other hand was searched and issued with a visitors pass before he was allowed in. It was quite a gathering; all the Heads of Armed Services were there, as well as the Heads of Homeland security, the CIA and the FBI.

Sitting up on the podium with the Senator, Milton looked at the chair beside him, wondering who'd be sharing the stage with them. A touch of his shoulder by the Senator made him stand. Looking around, he noticed that the whole room was now on their feet, as the President entered. Signaling for everyone to sit, he walked up onto the stage. Milton was awestruck as the Senator introduced him. Shaking his hand Milton mumbled a 'how are you Sir?' before they all sat down. The Senator then approached the microphone.

"The President and I have called you here today to disclose a secret breakthrough. It has occurred at one of our sponsored research facilities, run by my friend here

Dean Milton Campbell. What you hear here today will change the world as we know it." The Senator smiled, pointing to Milton to stand and approach the microphone.

"Gentlemen, to put it in simplified terms, a young scientist working on his thesis at our University, has made a breakthrough. He has managed to isolate the growth cells in the DNA of plant life. By genetically manipulating it, he can eradicate any plant life on the face of the Earth." Looking out at the audience Milton saw open bewilderment at what he was saying.

"Dumb it down a bit Dean. Give them an example," the Senator, besides him suggested. This received several chuckles from the audience.

"Let's put it this way. Say you wanted to stop a weed growing which was affecting your crops. You could drop a small 6-inch canister of this Blight anywhere in the country, and the target weed would be completely destroyed. This could be done without damaging any other plant life." Looking at the audience, he saw he wasn't getting through so he tried again.

"Or say you wanted to stop someone growing illegal drugs. Just by deploying a single vial which you could carry in your pocket, you could not only wipe out their entire illegal crops, but every other drug grower's crops on that continent." At first, the Dean thought they hadn't understood, when without warning a groundswell of voices erupted, as everyone started asking questions at the same time. The President standing brought silence again to the room.

"I think I speak for everyone here when I admit that this is beyond comprehension. Can this blight be used against commercial crops like wheat?"

"Yes Sir. Anything that grows can be targeted." Milton replied.

"My God, This could help mankind feed the world, or become the perfect weapon. Are we the only country working on it?" The President asked his voice sounding concerned.

"Yes Sir, Adrian's research is unique. No one else is even close."

"Good, I want this research, and this researcher locked down, until we work out a plan, for its use. Is your facility guarded?" The President asked, getting support from the assembly.

"Yes, Sir. Although we could use some more men and the scientist isn't an American."

"What! Where's he from?"

"Australia Sir, though he's American by birth." Dean Campbell hastily added.

"We can live with that. Have his passport confiscated and make sure he's guarded 24/7. And see that they get those extra men Dan." The President ordered, getting acknowledgement from Daniel Moore Head of the FBI.

"Gentlemen I want this kept buttoned up. There is no telling what might happen if other nations discover we have had this breakthrough." The President ordered, immediately leaving after giving the Dean a good work pat on the shoulder.

Dean Campbell became the flavour of the day, as everyone gathered in that room wanted to ask his opinion, on their take on the blights deployment. The military saw it as a way of punishing Rogue states. With it, they could destroy their enemy's ability to wage war from inside the sanctity of their borders. Homeland Security and the FBI saw it as a way of crippling the drug trade, which in some cases fuelled terrorism. The CIA, on the other hand,, remained silent.

Whatever they thought of the Blights use remained unclear. Milton wondered if they already knew about the research. After the meeting had broken up, Milton broached the subject of the CIA's silence.

"They're a shadowy bunch, I'll say that. They could have a mole working on the campus. I wouldn't put it past them." The Senator admitted watching the door.

"I could check the records we might find out who it is?"

"I'd forget it. Whoever it is, you'll never find them. They'd be buried too deep, best to just acknowledge they're there." the Senator chuckled.

"What do you think the President will do with this Blight?"

"It's an election year. He promised to hurt the drug cartels. I think he'll try it against them first. I would."

Darren Crammer yawning drove to the entrance of the Think-tank University. He was here on behalf of Homeland Security to assess their security procedures. For some reason unknown or secret, he'd been sent here to boost the University's protection. Why the FBI was treading on Homeland's turf worried him. Usually, they were quite uppity about the FBI interfering in their projects, meaning someone high up had ordered it.

He'd already looked at the schematics of the campus and had been impressed with the security already in place. Only in manpower could he see the need for an increase. It would give the staff the extra firepower, in the advent of trouble. There was one personnel problem he had with the place, and that was that arsehole Brett Heckle was working here. They'd been partners in an anti-drug unit in New York. Darren, in charge, was the senior agent.

Time in the job had made him cautious, while Brett was driven. Being just out of the academy, he was out to make a name for himself something Darren found worrying. They'd made several big busts together, but after some trouble, Brett started to work alone. On one of these unsanctioned raids, he'd singlehandedly smashed one of the biggest imports of heroin ever.

Darren had been furious, his anger came from the fact he hadn't been told of the bust. Brett had used the excuse that there was a rat in the office tipping off the drug lords. Darren like many other agents at the FBI was offended by Brett's accusation.

When a hit on Brett, killed his girlfriend instead of him, Darren headed up the investigation. Finding no leaks, the committee had put it down to Brett being careless, letting the druggie find out where he lived. Darren had also been completely exonerated of any wrongdoing. The committee also found no proof of a mole.

Brett had been less than impressed with the results. Drunk, he confronted Darren, which developed into an all-out brawl. Brett had been then indefinitely suspended over the incident. Their boss for some reason had helped him, getting him a babysitting job at the Think-tank, as a bodyguard. Now through a twist of fate, Darren would have to deal with the fool again. He hoped it went without incident.

Having a quick look around the campus perimeter, Darren turned his vehicle around driving back to LA. There he would meet up with his secretary Loraine at their hotel.

"Where is she?" Darren asked himself. Checking his watch, he saw that she was over three hours late. Loraine had been his secretary for over four years. When she had first been assigned to him, he'd been far from impressed. She had been slow with her reports and forgetful, causing several problems with cases he'd been in charge of.

Looks wise, she was plain, wearing shapeless clothing and large unattractive glasses, which dominated her face. Darren being married, at first had been glad that she wasn't too attractive, as this cut down on flirting, which was a problem in most offices. On one of his many trips around the country, Darren had taken Loraine to record statements from a group of informers. This helped convict a major crime figure, closing an important case.

For his work on the case, he received promotion and a well-deserved pay rise. Feeling on top of the world, Darren had asked Loraine out to dinner to celebrate. Meeting her in the restaurant in the hotel, where they were staying at, Darren before dinner had several celebratory drinks with the local agents. By the time Loraine arrived he'd consumed a fair load of alcohol.

When she walked into the restaurant, he at first had trouble recognising his mousy secretary. Gone were the glasses, replaced by contact lenses. Her usual shapeless clothes had been transformed into a tight fitting red dress, which showed off her long well-shaped legs. Darren was struck dumb. Unable to put two words together, he silently got up, pulling out her chair for her.

"Thank you, Darren." She smiled, kissing him slightly on the cheek before sitting down. Pushing the chair in behind her, Darren stared down at her cleavage, which revealed a braless pair of large firm breasts. Mumbling a 'you're welcome,' Darren sat down opposite her, as she smiled knowingly at his silence. At dinner, she admitted deliberately dressing down at work to fly under the radar of the male predators that stalked the secretarial pool.

Tonight she confessed dressing up for him, as she thought he deserved his promotion and she liked him.

Darren had been choked up by her confession. Thanking her for her praise they started their meal, talking about the case and work in general. After dinner, they moved to the bar having several more drinks. There was a dance floor adjoining the bar, so with Loraine's insistence, they both got up. The music was slow as they held each other close, their bodies moving with the rhythm against each other.

Loraine's perfume and Darren's excessive drinking made him more than aware of the young firm body woman dancing next to him. Lowering his hand down her back, he playfully grabbed her bottom.

"You flirt" She giggled, pushing her thighs against his crotch rubbing up against him.

They danced for another hour until Darren became unsteady. Loraine taking control steered him off the dance floor, supporting him. Reaching the lift, she led him inside holding him up, as the lift rose. Darren smiling playfully tried to kiss her on the neck, as Loraine giggled uncontrollably, showing she too had drunk too much.

"Settle down stud. With the amount you've drunk you couldn't perform if you wanted to." She laughed, as Darren thinking she was most probably right, chuckled. As the lift stopped, they both stumbled out holding each other for support.

"Where are your keys?" Loraine asked as Darren indicated his right pants pocket. Putting her hand in his pocket, she momentarily squeezed his crotch, before removing the keys. It was the most erotic thing that had been done to him in years, despite the alcohol, he felt his manhood swell. Watching him, a mischievous smile on the corner of her mouth, she opened the door moving in ahead of him.

"Cheeky." He grinned smacking on her arse, as she squealed, dropping the keys. As Loraine bent slowly down to retrieve them her dress rode up revealing she was wearing no underwear.

"Having a good look?" She asked softly, staying bent over as he moved forward. Pulling her up, he kissed her roughly on the lips, while pulling her against his growing member.

"Well, well, well." She giggled, thrusting herself upon him, rubbing against him. Breaking the kiss, he grabbed the front of her dress, ripping it down the middle. Her free breast jumped out teasing him, as he shoved his hands between her legs rubbing her sex. A moan escaped her, as she threw herself upon him kissing and biting him on the lower lip playfully. Pushing her to the floor, Darren swiftly stripped, while Loraine lay on the floor removing what was left of her dress. Naked he stared down at her as if admiring a prize.

"Are you just going to look at me stud?" She giggled, her hands circling her hard nipples, as she looked up at him, waiting. Bending down landing on his knees, Darren his eyes glazed with lust pulled her legs roughly apart and entered her.

It was the most explosive night he ever had. There was nothing he didn't make her do or try. Anything he'd ever wanted to do, but was afraid to ask of his wife he did, enjoying every minute of it. She, in turn, was unstoppable coaxing him on never wanting him to stop. They stayed the next day and night faking sickness, till in the end, they had to return to their lives.

Loraine knew he wouldn't leave his family, agreeing to a no questions asked affair, keeping it special. Darren thought he was the luckiest man alive. A click of the door heralded Loraine's arrival.

"Waiting long?" She asked dropping her suitcase by the door.

"Yes, I have. So crawl over here and take your punishment." He commanded. Smiling, Loraine slowly stripped till all that remained of her clothes, was her matching black silk bra and panties.

"I'm coming master." She giggled as she obediently she got down on all fours, moving slowly over to him.

"Now reach up and take off my pants. You've been bad." He smiled, as below him looking up Loraine dutifully undid his pants pulling them and his underpants off.

"Good slave," Darren smiled, before groaning with pleasure.

OLD FRIENDS

"What the fuck is Crammer doing here?" Brett shouted in the middle of Dean Campbell's briefing.

"Sit down and shut up Brett or you're fired. Do I make myself clear?" Milton shouted back, as the gathered security guards sat silently. "I know you've got history with this guy, but you will behave yourself or you're gone, that's it." Brett's hands clenched in a fist stood staring at Milton, before slowly sitting down.

"As I was saying, Darren Crammer is here to boost our security, relating to the breakthrough at the nursery." All of them knew something significant had occurred at the nursery, only Brett knew the full details.

"I didn't think the FBI had the power to put a whole team of regular agents here?" One guard asked, looking at Brett, knowing his history.

"Usually not, though this is something special men. I expect you all to give them any assistance they require. Am I understood?" When no one replied Milton left, giving Brett a follow me signal, as he passed him.

"Look, Brett, I know you've got a past with this guy, but Adrian's work is a big deal; we need the FBI's assistance.

"Yes I'm sorry boss; I was out of line back there. I just don't trust the guy." Milton stood watching Brett. He knew Brett's story and his allegation that someone, maybe Crammer was a mole.

"Look, Brett, if you can prove he's dirty I'll personnel help you bury the guy. Just give me something." Milton suggested patting Brett on the shoulder before walking away. Despite Milton's show of affection, he despised Brett, wanting him gone. He'd hoped to fire him with Andy, but he was scared how Adrian would react to either of them going. Since he had been officially told to remain on the campus Adrian had been less than friendly. So until he could find a way to stop Adrian kicking up a stink when he found out, he had to put up with both of these idiots.

The next day, Darren arrived with Loraine, for an inspection of the campus. He was personally, given a tour of the facility by the Dean Campbell. While walking, they discussed security aspects to improve the University's protection. The University to Darren's surprise had a state of the art secure computer network, the same as the Whitehouse and the Pentagon. Even the video surveillance system had face recognition over its extensive array of cameras throughout the campus.

Darren was impressed; the only area where improvement could be made was in manpower like he'd already worked out. After some light refreshments, he was introduced to the security team having a question and answer session feeling out the team. His only worry was waiting for Brett to chime in and try to fuck him up. For some reason, he'd remained attentive, causing no trouble.

Loraine, who sat to one side taking notes, had been worried by Brett presence here. She had confessed to Darren she was scared of him taking another swing at him. Giving her a smile showing everything was okay Darren decided to call it a day, asking if there were any last questions. One young man named Nathanial, towards the back shyly raised his hand.

"Are we in any danger from the discovery?" He asked which caused all movement in the room to stop.

"I'm sorry; I'm not privileged with that information."

"It's just that if it kills any type of plant what's to stop it killing us?" Nathanial continued.

"Silence! You are not to discuss the project at the nursery with anyone!" Dean Campbell shouted from the doorway. Pulling Nathanial from his seat, the Dean ordered him to his office, before turning to the others. "There is no danger to any person from the discovery. You will not discuss it further with anyone, is that understood!" The Dean ordered, before calming down. Darren embarrassed by the security slip remained silent, as across the room he saw Brett studying him.

"Look, I'm sure Nathanial didn't mean any harm men and our guests here have security clearance. That aside I can't begin to tell you how important this work is. Be on your guard men, it could save your life." Dean Campbell warned, leaving. With his departure, the room quickly cleared leaving Darren with Loraine.

"What was that all about?" She asked as Darren gathered up his papers.

"I'm not sure, though the Dean seemed rather upset."

"Anyway, it's nothing to do with us. Let's get back to the room." She smiled, playfully touching his thigh. As they were about to leave, the Dean reappeared pulling Darren aside, asking Loraine to wait in their car.

"I'd like to apologise for my outburst back there, it was uncalled for."

"Think nothing of it, Dean Campbell. I judge this project is important to you?"

"You've got no idea how big it is, the President himself is involved," Milton whispered.

"Is that why Homeland security is allowing us to reinforce the campus?"

"Yes, there will be quite a few angry people when the President acts." Dean Campbell chuckled.

"I judge it's got something to do with plants?" Darren asked, not really wanting to know. The Dean secretively looked around, dramatising how vital his information and he was.

"The blight we've invented can kill any type of plant growth we target. The President is about to wipe out the illegal drug industry." The Dean whispered, watching his reaction.

"My God, Do you know how dangerous it is to trust people with something like that!" Darren exploded.

"You're in charge of the FBI here; it's only a matter of time till you find out. I might as well tell you up front and then you'll know what you need."

"Tell no one else Dean and that includes my men. Does Brett know?"

"I wouldn't think so, although he's close to Adrian, the young scientist whose research led to this breakthrough."

"He's no fool if he knows the kid, he most probably knows everything. I'll get my team here pronto, and then we can seal the place up tight, just keep it quiet." Darren warned leaving. Walking to his car he saw Brett waiting, he instantly prepared for trouble.

"So they found a place for you?" Darren smiled, not being able to resist the barb.

"It's not too bad; at least here I can watch my back."

"I don't want any trouble, Brett. Just do your job, and we'll get along just fine." Darren replied watching Brett.

"If anything happens to that young scientist, I'll kill you," Brett promised his face devoid of emotion.

Ignoring the remark, Darren singled Loraine to drive over and pick him up. Brett seeing Loraine driving towards them turned and started to walk away.

"I can't believe you're still having an affair with her?" Brett said out loud, not turning back, as Darren surprised, stood staring after him.

Getting over Brett's comment, Darren jumped into the car, telling Loraine to drive. Pulling his phone out, he rung the LA office, wanting a ten-man team sent immediately to the campus. He then rang the New York office telling his boss the University needed urgent reinforcements. When his boss asked why he told him the President himself was involved. That ended any argument, his boss giving his support. Darren promised to send him a full report tomorrow via a secured data line.

Arriving at the hotel, Loraine went straight for a shower, while Darren prepared a brief for his boss. An hour later tired of waiting, Loraine appeared in front of him wearing a nothing but a small smile.

"I need attention too." She whispered leaning into him, kissing him.

"I'll be right there." he smiled, as he continued working.

"Must be important if I have to wait?"

"It's the biggest project I've ever been involved with. This will change the world." Darren told her his excitement evident.

"Well it's most probably top secret, so don't tell me." She giggled, giving him a seductive stance, before sauntering back to the bedroom. Darren watched her walk to the bedroom, any thought of work going. Locking his work in his briefcase, Darren got up and stripped off his clothes. Running in, he jumped onto the bed grabbing her, as she squealed in mock surprise. Wrestling her, he quickly pinned her down entering her as she playfully tried to resist him.

An hour later his body aching and covered with sweat, Darren got out of bed, walking to the bathroom. Turning the shower to just lukewarm he hopped in, reviving himself. He was just about to get out when Loraine hopped in beside him. He wondered where she got the energy as again she playfully grabbed him, using her hands to arouse him and again they made love.

Tired, so tired he could hardly carry her back to the bed; Darren collapsed entering a deep sleep. Loraine beside him watched him sleep before carefully sliding out from under him. Seeing he was sound asleep, she went to the dining table where he had been working. His notes weren't there, as like usual he had secured them in his briefcase.

It was a combination type case, popular with the agency for securing documents. It had a special feature, which when forced open incinerated the contents. Loraine had got it for him, even helped pick a unique code, the day they first made love. She used that code now to open it. Reading the documents, Loraine's exhilaration grew this was what she'd been waiting for, her big score.

Writing down Adrian's name and address at the University, she quickly wrote down an outline of his research. She then for her handler's sake pointed out where all the research was stored on the University's secure network computers located at the rear of the main Administration building.

This would be her retirement fund she smiled, as from the bedroom Darren called her name. Replacing the documents in the exact order she removed them, she locked the case before answering.

"Coming honey, I just visited the ladies room." She giggled. Walking back into the bedroom she found Darren resting on one arm waiting. Pushing him onto his back she straddled him, kissing him passionately, as Darren pulled her down onto him. She didn't have to fake being excited; she was more excited than she'd been in years.

All that money would soon be hers she thought, as reaching her first orgasm, she screamed with real joy.

CORTEZE

"Is this even possible?" Corteze asked, still unconvinced. Felix, his security advisor, nodded yes, after just having explained for the second time Dianna's information to him.

'What do I do?' Corteze thought to himself his eyes distant. Dianna had been working for them for over two years until now he hadn't had any doubts about her information, but this was something else. Felix believed her, he could see that, it was just the ramification this blight as they called it, would cause, could be horrific.

"How long do you think we have?" Corteze whispered his nervousness obvious.

"The President of America will want to use it before the next election, to fulfil his promise of crippling the drug smugglers. I'd say we have about a year as they will have to test it thoroughly, before deploying it."

"This could seriously hurt us, Felix, what do you suggest?"

"Stop the research and eliminate the researchers. Dianna has told us the scientist is working alone and gifted in this field. Stop him, and the project dies." Corteze stood thinking about it when an idea came.

"Maybe we're looking at it from the wrong angle. The Americans will, of course, use it against us, but I doubt they'd stop there. You did say the blight targets any plant didn't you?" Corteze asked

"Yes, that is what the report states."

"Then it can be used as a weapon against food crops as well. Imagine the power the person who possesses this blight will have. The Americans will do anything to keep it safe and away from their enemies."

"The other cartels won't be happy with you having this blight Corteze. They'll want it destroyed to guarantee their crops safety." Felix pointed out. He was secretly worried by his boss' new direction in wanting the blight.

"I was thinking the same thing, my friend. Arrange an emergency meeting of the Syndicate. Have them all come here to discuss the blight. Then we can settle the whole problem swiftly." Corteze smiled.

THE SYNDICATE

Mohamed Jamal stared out his window at the dense green jungle, feeling claustrophobic. 'Why did they call this meeting?' He asked himself. 20 hours ago he'd been driving through the open bleak mountain terrain of the Upper Swat valley. He'd been covered head to toe, trying to keep the endless swarms or flies and dust from choking him.

Now in Honduras, supposedly meeting his syndicate partners on neutral ground, he felt anything but safe. Sure Pakistan and Afghanistan were dangerous countries to live in, but you could see your enemy coming. Here the roads were lined with thick vegetation making spotting trouble impossible. He felt like a fish out of water.

"You can't see your enemy coming." He murmured softly out loud, feeling uneasy, as he asked himself again, 'why had he come?'

"I know how you feel Jamal. How can the infidels live here? I can feel my brain rotting just from the humidity." Kabal, his security advisor, replied smil ng as if sensing his boss's mood.

"It's supposed to be paradise?" Jamal smiled back, putting his reservations behind him.

"Maybe the infidels think it so. For myself, I prefer the barren mountains where you can feel God's presence." Raul, their chief accountant, exclaimed, as the others clapped in support.

"How do you want to handle this meeting?" Kabal asked, turning serious.

"It should be okay my brothers. At the moment we all need peace; it is beneficial to our shared business interest. Are the men ready anyway?" Jamal enquired as he glanced back at the small truck following their jeep. Inside were ten of Jamal's best men. Their job was to stay close, just in case, things didn't go to plan. As if they'd heard him speak, the truck suddenly slowed, turning off the road, disappearing into the surrounding jungle.

"They'll await your orders Jamal; I hope we don't need them," Kabal replied, knowing at the rendezvous they'd be outnumbered.

"As you said they are just infidels, money means everything to them." Jamal smiled, as the others laughed.

Ten minutes after the truck had turned off; they arrived at the hotel the syndicate had procured for this meeting. It had once been an exclusive hotel for the rich jet set Americans. Trouble with local guerrillas fighting for independence had strangled its business, till the local drug Cartel had purchased it. Restoring it to its former glory, it was now a retreat for a rich, if not more cautious patronage. It was also well protected, with several batteries of anti-aircraft missiles, plus a sizeable force of militia.

Driving up to the front entrance, Jamal's entourage was met by four porters, who took their bags if not their personal weapons. On hand to greet them was Corteze the local cartel leader and head of the South American drug syndicate.

"There is no need for weapons here my friends. But if it makes you more comfortable, you can carry them." Seeing no-one move to hand over their weapons, Corteze continued. I must warn you of one thing, if you break the truce, you will not leave here alive." Corteze told them pleasantly, the last part forcefully.

"Guns, where we are from, are part of getting dressed. I personally vouch for all my men." Jamal answered smiling.

"It seems we have not yet gained your complete trust Jamal, even so, be welcome. We have prepared food and drink to your liking.' Corteze smiled, leading the group inside.

Upon entering, Jamal found all twenty members of the Syndicate here, with their four security men and one business advisor. Each leader had been allowed a maximum of five men, by the room Jamal guessed everyone had brought the maximum. After Jamal's group being the last had taken refreshments, Corteze asked if everyone could take their seats in the conference room.

To Jamal's surprise, he found he had been given a prominent seat in the front row. This surprised him as at most meetings his group was at the rear. Corteze's group was to his right, while Son Tang's Asian group to his left. Son Tang next to Jamal had the most significant distribution network in the Syndicate. Jamal acknowledging him with a bow, received one in return.

There was something else Son Tang conveyed with his eyes, an air of uncertainty. Jamal had the impulse to move closer and find out what he knew. As he made to approach him, Felix the Syndicates intelligence officer stood, forcing him to sit down.

"Gentlemen, I have called this meeting to make you aware of a new weapon the Americans are about to unleash. The deployment of this weapon will lead to the end of growing all illegal crops from which we produce Heroin, Cocaine and Marijuana." At first, complete silence followed his statement as the Syndicate members digested what he had told them. Some after considering what had been said started to chuckle, thinking he was overstating the seriousness of the weapon.

"It is not a joke my friends or an exaggeration. Please continue Felix." Corteze shouted above the noise, silencing the gather men.

"I too was shocked by this development my comrades. My source inside the FBI has given me undeniable proof my friends. The American's have produced a disease or blight as they call it, which attacks any plant life they choose. A young scientist at a Think-tank University outside of Los Angeles has developed it. This new way of attacking plants is through their genetic code. A small vial of this blight can destroy all of the targeted plant life on an entire continent."

Jamal like many there, sat thinking about this new weapon. If it were true it would mean the end of growing drugs, but there was still pharmaceutical drugs produced in labs, these would survive. The problem was anyone with a backyard lab could make them, bringing an end to cartels like his, controlling supply. Looking across at Son Tang, he saw him nod to him, indicating he wanted to talk. Nodding in return, Jamal sat there as the noise of people talking grew in volume.

"How long before the Americans, can release this Blight?" Son Tang standing up asked, stopping the talk.

"At least one year. The blight must be thoroughly tested before being released. My person on the inside is keeping a close eye on its development" Felix answered.

"Then the research must be stopped at all cost!" another Cartel boss suggested.

"Our source is in place and can destroy the data recorded. Unfortunately, our source cannot get near the young scientist named Adrian Hayes; he is protected by the FBI."

"Then put a price on his head. Make it large enough to draw every hitman on the planet." Jamal suggested, getting support from the group.

"I'd suggest 5 million per member. It's more than enough to turn any man into an assassin." Corteze smiled. Jamal looked around the room seeing agreement, as everyone in the room clapped and applauded.

"God, for a hundred million dollars! Any Westerner would kill his own mother for that much money." Kabal beside him whispered. Jamal smiled, acknowledging his remark with a nod, but his mind was elsewhere. There was something else that had occurred to him about this development, something he needed to think about. Looking across the room, he saw Felix watching him, as Corteze stood up asking for silence.

When the room settled down, Corteze backed Jamal's idea, suggesting a vote. It was unanimous, so Corteze suggested that they all wire their funds to a Swiss bank account immediately. This would ensure that the money was in place, guaranteeing the successful assassin payment. He then asked for time so Felix could contact his people in LA to see if they could tell them anything more. Getting support for his idea the meeting broke up to reassemble at 8 that night.

As each cartel left the room, their business advisors stayed behind. These men arranged the transfer of their cartels 5 million dollars to the Swiss bank account, set up for the lucky assassin. As Jamal made to move away to their rooms, Son Tang appeared beside him.

"Be careful my friend, something is wrong here?" He whispered, moving away into the crowd, leaving Jamal wondering what he meant.

Walking to their suite, Jamal signalled for no questions until they arrived there. Once inside Kabal had the room swept for bugs, before asking Jamal what was going on?

"We must capture this scientist, not kill him," Jamal told him.

"I don't understand, you just had all the Cartels to put a price on his head."

"Forget about protecting the drug trade Kabal. Think of the victory, over America." Jamal exclaimed.

"I don't understand?"

"The weapon can destroy any crop, my friend, including American wheat and corn. We could achieve complete victory, while America starves. The Islamic world can become a reality." Jamal pointed out, seeing Kabal and the others get the message.

"God is great!" Kabal cheered, as all in the room joined in. After the celebrations had died down, Raul arrived. After Jamal told him what he planned, he voiced his concerns.

"The others here mightn't be too happy with our plan Jamal. It might be best to leave." Raul suggested. Jamal knew Raul was a born coward. He was also the most honest man he ever met. He had been with Jamal since the early days. In those days, someone at your back you could trust was the difference between life and death.

Seldom had Raul suggested a course of action. He was always happy to follow Jamal's lead, accepting whatever Jamal gave him. This made him speaking now, so important.

"What is wrong?" Jamal asked raising the hand for the others to be quiet.

"Corteze's cartel and a great many others here are happy taking scraps from the Americans. Surely they can see that this blight in their hands would give them immense bargaining power. I believe the hiring of assassin's to go after this scientist is a rouse to make us relax. I don't think they intend to let us leave here Jamal. They know our true following is Islam, not money."

"We're talking about hundred million dollars, Raul. Surely they are serious about killing him." Jamal pointed out.

"I don't think they care either way. It's the data they're after." Jamal went silent thinking over what Raul had said and earlier Son Tang's warning. Making a decision, he wondered if it was too late. Going to the window, Jamal looked out over the jungle. He then stared down seeing a drop of sixty feet below him.

"I wondered why they gave us the Presidential suite and not Corteze. It wasn't respect; it was because we are trapped in this room. Raul is right, we must leave immediately. It's either fight our way out, or we die." Jamal told them all, as Kabal ran to his bag.

"Not necessarily." Kabal smiled pulling out the contents, which consisted of a coil of rope.

"How did you know?"

"I didn't. I just had each of the men bring something different. I decided on rope, because back home we always carry some."

Opening up the four bags carried by his men Jamal found, a first aid kit, spare ammunition for their pistols, and a radio. Raul, of course, had brought financial papers nothing else. Moving to the window, Kabal quickly checked the surrounding area before securing the rope and throwing it over the side. One by one, the six men descended to the ground.

Once they had all abseiled down, they swiftly moved into the jungle. Here Kabal radioed their back up men, warning them they were coming to their position. Jamal looking back at the hotel saw Son Tang standing on his balcony looking down at him. Signalling to him that he should leave, Son Tang smiling, pointed to the drop from his balcony.

Unlike his men, Son Tangs men hadn't allowed for the drop. Calling to one of his men, Jamal had him pulled down their rope and throw it to Son Tang. Once Jamal saw they had caught it, he led his men into the jungle. They'd been moving for twenty minutes when the unmistakable sound of gunfire erupted behind them.

"We owe you all our lives, Raul. From now on we are brothers.' Jamal declared as each man, in turn, came forward, thanking him. Knowing time was critical, Jamal told Kabal to lead them to his reserve soldiers. Kabal nodding his understanding, cautiously moved away from the hotel, moving parallel to the road they'd come in on.

Corteze stood with his men examining the dead Syndicate members. It was sad to kill all the other leaders, but his plans didn't include sharing. When Felix had told him of the blight and the power that could be controlled by possessing it, they had decided to end the agreement. Since Corteze controlled the hotel, it had been easy to lure all the leaders here, allowing for them to bring only a few men.

All had gone to plan; only Son Tang and Jamal's groups were missing. Both were canny men, they must have seen it the same way as he had. With fifty miles of jungle between the hotel and the nearest town of any worth, Corteze was still confident. Alerting the local militia, which he had influence over, Corteze announced a bounty of a fifty thousand US dollars a head.

Already over two hundred of his men and over five hundred soldiers and militiamen were out scouring the countryside. He knew it wouldn't take long to find them.

"What do you think Felix?" Corteze asked.

"Jamal worries me more than Son Tang, they were prepared.

"We know he brought extra men, maybe he thinks to fight his way out?" Corteze suggested.

"Maybe, though we know that's not going to happen." Felix smiled.

Jamal and his men slowly closed on the position where he had left his men. They'd tried several times to contact them on their radio. Only static answered their calls.

"I don't like it, Jamal. They would've answered us if they lived. I'm afraid they have been eliminated." Kabal confessed.

"We must know for sure. They are my men I will not abandon them."

"Let me go ahead? If everything is okay, I will return to you." Kabal volunteered.

"You are too valuable to me my friend, choose another," Jamal ordered. Turning to his men Kabal asked for someone to go, Raul was the only one who didn't beg to be sent, which made the others smile. In the end, he sent Calla, mainly because he was the most expendable. Smiling as if he'd won the lottery Calla hurried off, feeling proud he'd been chosen to prove himself.

Moving back away from the road they waited patiently for news. Calla hadn't been gone five minutes when an avalanche of shots rang out.

"They are close Jamal, we must move away from this road," Kabal whispered, as the group swiftly moved into the surrounding jungle. Stopping, Jamal pulled out a map of the local area. To their north was the road running east to west. West was the hotel surrounded by dense jungle. To the east was civilization which by now was crawling with Cortez's men. South seemed the only option. It did lead to several large cities; the problem was it was through dense jungle.

"We can make it, but it will take several weeks, and we have only basic equipment, and no food," Jamal told the others.

"Do we have another choice I didn't bring my boots?" Kabal smiled, looking down at his leather shoes.

"I'll buy you another pair my friend when we get out of here." Jamal chuckled softly, getting suppressed laughter from his men

"Or you can come with us!" Son Tang voice whispered through the surrounding jungle, making everyone dived for cover, except Jamal. "Relax gentlemen if I wanted you dead you would be." Son Tang reassured them as he emerged from the dense growth. Once Jamal men had gotten over the shock they stood up with Jamal.

"I suppose you're at home here in this green hell?" Jamal smiled.

"Yes, its similar to the Golden Triangle, though I wish was there now." Son Tang smiled back.

"I judge there's a reason for saving us?" Jamal asked.

"Yes, my friend. While making our escape, one of my men was hit. We couldn't leave him behind, so we were forced to kill him. He was my pilot."

"So you have a plane or a chopper here somewhere. What's it to us?"

"I remembered your man Raul flew you to a meeting, we had last year in Hong Kong. I thought for taking you with us, we could form a partnership of mutual friendship until we're away from here."

"I always liked you Son Tang, you have a way of stating the obvious." Jamal chuckled.

"Then I suggest we get moving." Son Tang smiled, surprising them by heading back the way they had come. Jamal was amazed and slightly suspicious that he would head towards his meeting place with his men. Kabal, he could see to was on edge, sensing a trap. As if picking up their concerns Son Tang stopped.

He explained how now the trap had been sprung, Cortez's men would've already moved from their positions to flank Jamal's men to the south. He knew it was the only direction unprotected, so he'd sent his men south to cut them off. Jamal could see a grudging admiration in Kabal for Son Tang, for his grasp of tactic.

After travelling for over four hours Son Tang called a halt for the night, setting up a cold camp, meaning no fires. It was a miserable night, as the mosquitoes attacked relentlessly making sleep near impossible. By morning even Son Tang's men look exhausted, as again they moved off.

"It amazes me how you brought a plane in here?" Jamal admitted, walking beside Son Tang.

"I didn't, we'll be taking one of Cortez's planes." He informed him, stopping Jamal in his tracks.

"How are we doing that?"

"He flies his drugs out to America from a hidden airfield a couple of clicks ahead. The reason I know this, is that one of his former pilots who stole a shipment from him. Needing somewhere to hide, after Corteze found out, he came to me. Corteze thinks the man dead so he won't be expecting it."

"I hope you're right, or it will have been a long walk for nothing if you're wrong." Jamal pointed out. "By the way, what happened to the pilot?"

"I had him killed. It would be a bad example for our employees to think they could steal from us and get away with it."

The arrival at the airstrip was an anti-climax. True to his word Jamal found two planes sitting quietly, under an elaborate structure made up of camouflage nets. From the air, the airstrip looked abandoned, with what appeared to be derelict machinery and burnt out planes at the far end of the runway. It was only when you approached from the ground, that the truth could be seen. It was all fabricated, while the true buildings and machine shops were set back in the jungle with a colossal camouflage net covering the entire area.

Splitting the men into two groups, they approached the buildings from opposite sides, catching the men inside in a deadly crossfire. It was over swiftly as only four men were stationed here. Running to the planes, the nets were pulled back, allowing the aircraft to be checked, before moving them out onto the runway. The larger plane was an old twin-engine Dakota, which could comfortably hold up to thirty people. Raul picked this one, as it had the legs to fly them to a safe destination in Mexico, if not America.

Raul was just about to test the engines when the sounds of approaching vehicles cut short his pre-flight check. Yelling for everyone to get on board, Son Tang still in the maintenance shed, upended several drums of fuel, before running for the plane. Scrambling aboard, he looked back, as the first vehicle neared the maintenance area. Grabbing a flare he taken from the shed, he ignited it, throwing it back towards the shed. As the Dakota roared to life, the whole plane shuddered, as with a loud thump the maintenance shed exploded.

The fuel had ignited, sending flames and debris rocketing into the air. As the fire spread, it consumed everything combustible, as a thick black cloud of smoke billowed out of the burning structures. This was what Son Tang had planned, blocking the vehicles view of the accelerating plane. By the time they'd worked their way around the fire and smoke, the aircraft was airborne and out of range.

For the next eight hours, Raul flew north skimming first the mountains then the ocean. Approaching the Mexico coastline, he kept on the deck, even though from experience he knew the authorities here were less than vigilant. Once inside Mexico airspace, Raul worked his way through the interior mountain range, which was called the Rocky Mountains on the American side.

Running low on gas Raul landed the plane, twenty miles short of the border with America, on a disused airstrip. Both parties keeping their word, departed as friends, going their separate ways. Jamal even wished Son Tang good luck, each man giving the other a knowing smile as they shook hands. Each leader knew the other would try for the scientist or the data, but for now, the truce held.

Son Tang's group departed first, after procuring a serviceable vehicle from an unfortunate farmer. He'd made the mistake of stopping, to see what was going on, a fatal mistake. Jamal watching them disappear down a winding dirt road ordered his group to return to the airfield.

"Why return to the field?" Kabal asked surprised.

"I didn't land here by chance Kabal. This is one of our drop-off points for our deliveries. There's fuel for the plane buried here." Raul informed him. Making sure the area was indeed empty; Jamal had his men recover several fuel drums buried beside the runway, near an abandoned hangar. Once refuelled, they flew the plane towards the border.

"This is dangerous Jamal. Flying here was relatively easy compared to crossing the American border." Raul warned sensing danger, making Jamal smile.

"We'll cross low and land the plane in the desert as soon as possible. I have already contacted some of our people in the states. They with luck will pick us up once we land. Don't worry my friend, God is with us."

"Do you think Son Tang will try for the scientist?" Raul asked changing the subject.

"I'd say he's on the way there now," Jamal admitted liking the man.

"I have to admit Son Tang impressed me," Kabal admitted.

"What if we meet again when we try for the blight?" Jamal asked seriously.

"Then he, with God's will, shall travel on to the next life."

CIA HEADQUARTERS VIRGINIA

Liam sat at his desk listening to the rap music on his iPod. He wasn't sure he really liked rap music, but several girls in the office did, so he decided to play along. The words were hard to follow on his pirated copy, but the beat was good as he thumped out a tune on his desk. He'd been given the dead shift supposedly, 'for being on the ball.' His boss had told him it was his big break, although it didn't seem so at the moment.

9 in the night till 7 in the morning, was the dead shift, the time when everyone with some common sense was asleep. Seeing it was nearing the hour, Liam took off his headset preparing for the test.

On the hour a random code would appear on the screen in front of him. This was to check if he was awake and at his station. He upon receiving it would have to enter the same code on his keyboard, or an alarm would sound summing security. Once it had happened while he was in the can taking a dump, it had been most embarrassing.

He'd been dragged out by security with his pants around his ankles, getting a lecture from the female soldier in charge. Smiling about it, Liam looked down to see the codeword flash spelling 'arse wipe.'

"Some fuck's got a funny sense of humour." He growled, typing in the code. That was the third time they'd used those words making Liam fume.

Forgetting it, he went through his checks, making sure the equipment was in working order. What he was doing didn't look very exciting. If someone could have looked into the windowless room, they would have been, to say the least, unimpressed. The room for all intense and purpose was just a desk, a coffee machine and an oversized computer.

But no one was going to have a casual look at this room, as the security to get to this below-ground bunker was the best in the world. This room was nicknamed the 'The Brain' by the personnel stationed here. Its very existence was kept secret. It was the Intelligence transmitting and receiving office, where all CIA assets and agents sent their Intel from all over the world.

Using the latest in high-speed burst transmissions chips, a message the size of a small novel could be sent in a fraction of a second. Most information received was about unconfirmed enemy movements, suspected terrorist locations and intentions. It also contained general information on threats to America or its allies by economic or political means. Once received, the reports would be checked and rechecked before a suitable action or response could be prepared.

These went through Liam's console without him lifting a finger. His job was to watch for 'Flash burst', critical information on operations happening real time. This type of message would only be sent by undercover agents, or totally reliable asset when something big was happening. Once received, they were immediately acted upon. He'd been doing this shift for over two weeks and in that time hadn't seen any of these burst. He started to wonder if anyone was really out there doing anything.

Tired of the iPod music and being bored, he got up stretching, before walking to his coffee machine. Boiling some water, he was just adding the milk, when the console behind him went into meltdown. 'Flash Burst' flickered on the screen in large letters as an ear piercing siren sounded.

Dropping his coffee down the front of his pants in surprise, Liam let out a scream of pain, rushing back to the desk. His crotch was on fire as between tears, he read the message decoding on the screen. Kicking off his shoes he ripped his pants off, all the time watching the message.

"Bloody Hell!" he screamed reading of a coming attack in LA. Remembering his operating procedure, he picked up the phone, calling the Directors special number.

By the time Director Milton Douglas walked in, the situation room was flooded with staff. One of his two secretaries, named Suzy, immediately brought him up to speed. While this was going on, he couldn't help noticing the young man wearing a towel around his waist.

"Who is that?" He asked her.

"His name is Liam. He received the burst while making a cup of coffee. He upended his cup scolding himself, while rushing back to the console." She giggled softly.

"Give him a well done. It must have hurt?" He smiled moving on. Going over the information from their deep cover agent, Milton saw the gravity of the situation.

"Your attention please!" He shouted, getting immediate silence. "We have a large group of people heading to America to do harm to someone working for our country's national interest. He's located outside of LA in a Thinktank University. This is a chance to do some real good. I want as many of these bad guys intercepted as possible. Cancel all leave; I want everyone we can recruit, working on this pronto. I also want a group set up to find who leaked this information.

The meeting where this project was discussed with the President was just under three weeks ago. Check out everyone at that meeting, and anyone involved afterwards. Also, call the University; warn them they've got trouble coming their way. Get on it now people!" He ordered, as his staff rushed off in every direction.

Turning to his secretary, he told her to arrange a meeting with the President.

"It's four in the morning Sir." Suzy reminded him.

"Wake him up."

Darren exhausted lay beside Loraine when his phone started ringing. God, she was killing him he smiled, remembering the night, as he grabbed his phone. Darren nearly jumped from his bed when the FBI director himself came on the line.

"Someone leaked the information to the Cartels. They have put a price on Adrian Hayes head of a hundred million, can you believe that?"

"Where'd the leak come from?" Darren asked, as beside Loraine lay silently listening.

"We're not sure yet, but get to the University pronto. There's no telling when someone might take a run at that scientist." Darren springing out of bed dialled the University security, checking if they knew. After reassuring him that everyone was on alert, he started dressing.

"What's going on?" Loraine asked yawning.

"The druggies have found out about the project, they've put a price on the scientist's head. I've got to run."

"Are you sure? It could be just another rumour."

"No way, the CIA has got someone inside the Cartel. It's legit." He explained moving for the door, leaving Loraine lying silently behind him.

Once Darren had left Loraine staggered to the bathroom throwing up. They could be coming for her at any minute she contemplated nervously. Running to her phone, she started to dial a prearranged number, given to her by Felix. Stopping, she deleted the number, wondering if the CIA or the FBI could be monitoring her phone number already. Looking at her watch, she realised the bomb she'd planted at the University's mainframe still had three hours to run, there was still time to get away.

Two days ago Felix had contacted her giving her an address. Telling Darren she was unwell, he'd left her at the unit, while he went to the university. Meeting her contact, he had given her an ordinary looking laptop, a perfect match for her own.

His instructions were simple. Log into the secure network at the University and let the laptop do the rest. Once connected to the system, it would download the scientist's data, placing it onto what looked like a small USB stick. When it finished loading the data, all she had to do was remove the stick and leave the laptop connected.

When the preset time arrived, or someone tried to disconnect the laptop, it would trigger an electronic blast. This would fry all electronics in the area and at the same time be harmless to people. As instructed, she had connected the laptop the day before, setting the time for 10am the next morning. She had also downloaded the data onto the stick; she had that with her now.

She planned to go with Darren to work that morning and be there to make sure the computer network, was wiped out. Once she had confirmed its detonation, she would've faked some illness and return to the hotel. She had hoped in the panic that would follow the detonation, her laptop would appear to be just collateral damage. Now they knew that the cartel had someone on the inside, they'd look for the source of the explosion straight away.

"I hope the Cartel finds that scumbag CIA mole and give him what he deserves." She said out loud when it occurred to her that she was exactly the same type of scumbag, maybe even worse. Putting it behind her, she raced to the closet, throwing her clothing into her bag. Writing a quick note to Darren she left it on the table, before rushing out of the apartment.

Since Darren was here on a semi-permanent basis, Loraine had been supplied with her own car. Taking it now she drove away from LA, heading inland. Driving east for an hour she pulled up at a small gas station. Filling up she used their public phone, ringing her contact. To her surprise, Felix answered himself.

"Loraine, how did it go, did you copy the files?"

"Yes I did, and I've been blown. Someone in your fucking organisation tipped the CIA off. I planted the laptop yesterday as planned, in two hours the network will be gone and I expect to be paid." She demanded.

"Are you sure it was someone inside our cartel?" Felix was surprised.

"Yes. The FBI chief himself rang Darren to warn him. I'm sure."

"I am sorry Loraine, we are grateful for your help. I suggest not using your credit cards that you have in your name. Use the alternatives we gave you. We'll arrange to meet and pick up the files once you're safe. Good luck." Felix's assuring voice calmed her.

"Thanks, Felix it's been a rush." She giggled, hanging up feeling better. "Now all I have to do is get to the border and cross it." She smiled, turning north.

Felix stared at the phone worried. Someone had tipped the CIA off. It was unlikely it was one of their people, but

Felix couldn't be a hundred percent sure. That left only Son Tang's and Jamal's men, as all the others at the meeting were dead. For now, Felix decided to keep this information from Corteze.

He was already unimpressed at his ability to control security, now this. Picking up his phone again he contacted two of his men. Giving them instructions on where he thought Loraine was headed, he ordered them to make sure they retrieved the USB stick from her no matter what the risk.

As Darren arrived at the University, he saw a steady stream of cars filled with students leaving. Approaching the guard station, he saw extra security posted at the entrance. Taking his turn, he moved up the queue. Recognizing him they waved him through. Instead he pulled over. Checking the gate entrance, making sure his men were in position, he approached one of the gate guards.

"Why is everyone leaving?"

"The Dean made an announcement that an angry student may have brought a gun to the campus. He suggested everyone take the week off and return after the weekend." The guard told him.

"Clever, is everyone on duty?"

"Yeah, they're expecting you." The guard replied.

There was something about the way he said it, that made Darren wary. As he drove towards the admin building, Darren noticed more than one agent look towards him then turn away. It suddenly twigged that Brett may have told them about him being dirty and that he might be the leak.

Arriving at the admin building, he saw Brett standing with Dean Campbell, waiting.

"What's up?" Darren asked defensively.

"The FBI just rang. The leak came from here. They checked the time against the information. Only someone here knew the project was being run by a young scientist named Adrian Hayes." Silence settled on the group as the three men waited for someone to say something, in the end, Brett spoke.

"Look the message said they'd try for Adrian, as well as the network containing his data. We have to go on the assumption that they could already have something running. I've suggested a search of the computer area, plus we move Adrian." Darren stood there staring at Brett. He'd expected him to attack him as the leak.

"You okay Darren?" Milton asked.

"Yeah just chewing over what Brett said. Sounds like a good plan, I'll send some of my men to carry out a search."

"Okay, get on it, but Adrian stays here, his research must be finished," Milton told them.

"That could be dangerous, for" Brett started to say, Milton angrily cut him off.

"I'm willing to risk it. He's safer here, and we have the data just in case." Milton pointed out. Darren saw Brett bristle up. He was just about to have a go at the Dean when Darren put out his hand stopping him.

"Brett, come with me, we'll check the computer room." He suggested, leading Brett away. The two men left the Dean standing there, as they hurried towards the computer area.

"Thanks back there, I nearly lost it," Brett admitted.

"That's okay, the guys a dick. You know for a moment back there, I thought you were going to accuse me of being the mole?"

"It had crossed my mind, but it's too easy, you're cleverer than that." Brett smiled.

"I couldn't blame you, it looks bad. Must be one of my men or a guard here, no one else knows.'

"Yeah, it's a mystery. We'll worry about it later, let's secure the computers first." Arriving at the room, which was more like a shopping centre than a control room, Brett and Darren joined the search. Twenty minutes of searching each of the massive mainframes found nothing out of the ordinary. Returning to the main control area Brett had Brenan do a complete sweep of the programs looking for any viruses inside the system.

It took ten minutes to scan the entire system; in the end, it showed only one virus.

"Sorry gentlemen, there's nothing to report," Brenan answered.

"Are you sure, it shows a virus?"

"It always has. Ever since Adrian Hayes loaded his new program to our network, it's shown a virus. His program is like nothing anyone has seen before, so the software thinks it's a virus. Look I'd know if anything else were wrong, my friends. The only two things registering a signal at the moment are my PC and Loraine's at her desk over there. She must've left it on yesterday when she left?" Brenan smiled.

"Disconnect it now!" Brett suddenly screamed, running towards the laptop. Darren perplexed, wondered what he was doing when a thought erupted in the back of his mind. Brenan reacting to Brett's shouting, immediately typed in the shutdown code, cutting Loraine's PC from the network. It was all to no avail, as the laptop suddenly blew apart, plunging the room into darkness. Everything went out, the power, the computers, the phones, even their mobiles were fried.

"What the hell just happened?" Darren shouted as emergency lighting flickered on.

"Someone just used an electromagnetic pulse or an EMP weapon," Brenan answered. "It fries electrical systems, I'm afraid we've got a complete write off here of our network."

"Do you have a backup system?" Brett asked.

"No, not really, we never saw a need for what we've got here. We're safe though, last week the Dean made me copy the complete data system and upload it to a government server in Washington. It was lucky he insisted, I myself thought we were safe here, nearly didn't do it." Brenan admitted.

With the emergency lights giving something to work with, Brett examined Loraine's laptop. Though completely burnt out, Brenan positively identified it as the EMP. Darren couldn't find the words, as he desperately tried to come up with something to clear Loraine. She'd use him, he felt like a complete idiot. Looking at Brett, he saw in his eyes he now knew who had arranged the killing of his girlfriend.

"I'm so sorry Brett." He managed to get out, as he wiped tears from his eyes. Brett was just about to answer when Dean Campbell burst into the room. Brenan had told him what had happened showing him Loraine's laptop.

"You're finished, Crammer. That whore of yours has screwed the whole complex. I want you off the campus immediately!" Milton shouted; bringing the whole room to a stop.

"Take it easy Milton, Darren is still in charge." Brett reminded him.

"Not once I get a working phone." Milton spat out, walking outside.

"I'm going after her Brett. You're in charge till I return." Darren told him sadly.

"For what it's worth, I don't blame you," Brett told him offering his hand. Darren pulling himself together shook Brett's hand with the two of his. Unable to say anything else to Brett, Darren left, running to the car park. Going from car to car, he tried four, before he found one that worked. Starting it, he slammed it into gear, screaming out of the car park. Driving to the front gate, he slammed on the brakes stopping.

"Has anyone got a working phone?" He called out. Finding one guard had one that worked. Darren rang his head office bringing them up to speed. Thinking there was a small chance Loraine might still be at the unit, he jumped back in his car driving there.

Racing into the unit, drawing his gun, he found she'd gone. He was just about to leave, when he saw the note, it was her confession. She didn't try to make up an excuse, confessing she had done it for the money. They'd told her the information she supplied, would only be used to stop the authorities from intercepting their men and drugs. At no time was she involved in Brett's girlfriend's murder, they'd got that info from another source inside the police force.

Loraine told him she loved him and hoped someday he'd forgive her. Darren sat down sobbing, before screwing the note up cursing and screaming in anger.

Ringing the office, he asked them to use the tracking chip installed in all FBI cars to pinpoint hers, having noticed it was missing. It came back with her near the border with Canada near the Seattle crossing. Telling them to stop her there, he ran to his car, flattened the accelerator. Turning on his blue lights and sirens, he drove like a madman wondering what he'd do when he reached the border.

THE ATTEMPT

Two hours before the EMP pulse went off; Adrian was in his lab checking the results of his blight. It was going to plan he thought, as out of the corner of his eye he saw two guards take up station, outside his door. Twenty minutes later, Brett arrived.

"What's going on Brett?"

"Look I shouldn't say anything, but it seems someone leaked your research to the wrong people. We've been warned someone might try to stop you."

"You mean kill me don't you?" Adrian replied angrily, as Brett stood there feeling useless. 'Do you think I should get out of here now?"

"No, security is tight at the moment you're safer here than trying to leave. I'll tell you when it's time to go." Brett whispered watching the door.

"Thanks, that's the first time you've been on my side for awhile."

"Don't get all sloppy on me, just be careful. You're supposed to be a genius, work out how to disappear if you have to." He suggested. Moving to the door, Brett gave him a wink, before going to meet Darren and the Dean.

Finished loading data onto the network server found Adrian thinking about his options. Leaving the campus would not be easy. Surveillance was pretty tight, so he'd have to work out where best to leave from. Looking around the room, his eyes came to rest on a service duct at the rear of his lab. He was just moving towards it, when the lights without warning, went out.

Total darkness descended on the whole complex, as Adrian froze fearing the worst. Seconds later the emergency power kicked in. Adrian was relieved, immediately, thought of his upload. Moving back to his workstation, he started to check his research, when the two guards outside, started banging on his door. Walking to it, he found the electric lock wouldn't budge.

Assuring them he was alright, he found they'd lost communications with their control room. Suggesting one of them go find out what had happened, he continued checking his data. It was all there he smiled, making sure the program was running correctly before logging off. Looking again at the service duct, Adrian went through several different scenarios for getting away.

Twenty minutes passed before the guard returned. He informed Adrian about the EMP weapon being used. Both guards seemed worried as if the use of the weapon heralded impending doom. Taking up their positions again talking amongst themselves, Adrian returned to his research. In the back of his mind, he still thought about leaving straight away.

Reluctantly, he decided to wait, until Brett signalled that it was time. Finished compiling information he was just about to call it a day when a red light flickered across his screen. Looking closely, he saw it was reflecting onto the computer screen from his clothing. Looking down, he saw a small red dot on the front of his shirt, roughly where his heart was. It was then that he heard the bang.

The ASSASSIN

Ian Johnson was at home in his apartment in LA, when the contract appeared on the screen of his laptop. Retired from the Marines after being injured by a roadside bomb in Iraq, the former sniper had gone freelance. Now for the right price, he took assignments that paid a lot better than the Marine's disability pension did? Looking at the decoded message, he at first thought there was a mistake.

'Someone had put too many zeros on the contract,' he surmised, sending a reply, asking confirmation. There was no mistake the return message informed him. The hit had a payday of a hundred million. 'Shit this was too good to be true' he smiled, writing down the local address and description of the target. The contract looked pretty straightforward; the only thing that worried him was it was inside America.

Up until now, he had a golden rule of only taking contracts overseas. The amount of money changed that. Accepting the contract by coded email, he went to his local library. Looking up the Think Tank University, he got its location. Once he had the position, he Googled the University's schismatics, getting a layout of the buildings. Happy with the information, he then researched Adrian, getting a personal photo from his article in the paper, on plant genetics. Having achieved his objectives, he returned home.

Going to his garage he removed a fake wall panel, revealing a hidden room. Moving inside he turned off the security system before opening his safe. The inside was arranged into ten shelves. The top seven contained large amounts of money stacked in bundles. The three bottom shelves contained weapons. Reaching down he removed a Browning 9mm handgun, loading it.

Placing it in his belt behind his back, he covered it with his shirt. On the bottom shelf, he removed an oversized briefcase. Opening it, he looked over his dismantled, much-loved weapon. Taking one piece out at a time, he slowly assembled it.The Barrett 50 calibre sniper rifle, was the same weapon he'd used in Iraq. Holding it lovingly, he cradled it in his arms applying a thin coating of oil. Wiping it clean afterwards, he checked the weapon's mechanism making sure it functioned correctly. Satisfied with its condition, he packed it into a canvas sleeve, propping it against the wall.

Going to a cupboard alongside the safe, he removed a haversack, loading it with supplies from the same closet and some ammo. He also packed a camouflage suit called a Gillis, this too he'd used in Iraq. Securing it to the top of the pack, he loaded his gear into his four-wheel drive.

Making sure no one was watching him; he drove out of his garage, parking in the street. Checking once more to be safe, that he had all he needed, he left for the University, looking forward to a big payday.

Driving to the base of the mountain range behind the University, Ian parked his vehicle off the road on a seldom-used dirt track. Switching to four-wheel drive, he drove up into the hills, parking in a ravine. Throwing a camouflaged net over his vehicle, he made sure it was well hidden. Donning his Gillie suit over his body and pack, he moved off up into mountains.

It took him all of the morning to get up on the ridgeline above the Uni. By the time he'd made it to the top, his back was throbbing with pain. A piece of shrapnel still embedded near his spine, reminded him of why he'd been sent home, from Iraq. Keeping his silhouette veiled, he moved cautiously along the ridge just below the crest of the hills, looking for a spot to set up. He'd tried several spots, looking for the perfect position for the shot, while staying hidden.

Knowing from the blueprints that the labs were in the southern area of the Campus, he moved closer to that area. Finding at last on his fourth try an ideal location, he prepared his firing pit. Digging a shallow scrap, he lay down in it, covering the whole area with camouflage netting. In his Gillis suit already, he was sure no one could spot him, but you could never be too sure. It was the same reason he had dug the pit. It had nothing to do with being shot at; the purpose was to prevent his muzzle flash from being spotted.

Looking through his spotter scope he searched for his target, believing he'd be working somewhere in Labs building. On his fifth sweep, he spotted him. Adrian was in his chair, facing the window as he worked on his laptop. With the scope, he checked the wind speed and distance writing them down. Putting the scope back in his pack, he picked up the Barrett.

Focusing on Adrian's window, he loaded three rounds. Lining up the target, he adjusted his range to what he'd recorded, noting it was just under a thousand yards. Because of the high winds, he decided on a chest shot, rather than miss at this distance. Relaxing his breathing, he took three breaths to steady himself. Pressing the small button above his trigger activated his red dot. The infrared targeting system gave him to the inch, the point of impact. Confident he slowly squeezed the trigger.

When the bang sounded, Adrian jumped at the noise but didn't react. Ian on the hill above him looked from his rifle to the still alive Adrian. The shot he concluded hadn't penetrated the glass window. It was the bullet striking the glass, which produced the bang. 'Some type of bulletproof glass' Ian concluded, before firing again.

Adrian still surprised by the noise looked to the window, as the security guards outside started hammering on his door. This time he saw and heard the bullet impact. Unlike before when the shot failed to penetrate, this time the glass shattered resembling a spider's web, as small pieces broke free.

"Get down!" A guard outside screamed, knowing exactly what the sound was. Adrian obeying dropped to the floor. It saved his life, as a third bullet penetrated the glass, exploding into the wall behind his seat. Ian on the hill looked at the room through his scope, seeing Adrian crawl away out of his view.

"You've got nine lives, my friend." He smiled, picking up his weapon. Slowly he turned around, inching his way on his belly back over the rise. 'I've just blown a hundred million bucks', he told himself, following his mission parameters. 'Always protect your own arse,' he'd been told during training. He knew that after three shots, his position was known. Sure he could stay and reacquire the target, but the chances were, he'd be spotted.

You couldn't spend the money if you were in prison or dead, so retreating was the only option. He'd just started to leave his pit when a blur of movement to his right made him freeze.

"Are you okay Adrian?" Michael, one of the two guards outside his door asked, as they both entered, keeping away from the window.

"Yeah, though I'm glad the windows are explosive resistant," Adrian replied shakily.

"I didn't know we had glass like that?" Brody admitted looking at the window, as shots sounded from the hills above them, making them all duck back down.

"They're fitted on all the labs, just in case our experiments go wrong. Guess they stop bullets just as well?" Adrian told him.

"Not all the time." The other guard smiled, making them all laugh, relieving the pressure.

When a frantic Brett and his team arrived, the first sound they heard was laughter. Wondering what the hell was going on, the team charged in. They found Adrian and the two guards lying on the floor chuckling.

"Are you all okay?" Brett inquired, looking at the shattered window, as the sound of shots being fired sounded from the hills above them.

"We are now. Did the other team get the shooter?" Brody asked.

"They're not our guys shooting out there my friend. We don't know who's up there." Brett answered, silencing the room as the sound of gunfire receded.

Brett's team stayed with Adrian for the rest of the day. Two hours after the initial shooting two Police choppers searched the hills, finding nothing. Being as it was getting towards dark, they decided on a more thorough search the following morning. Brett watched the window with a growing sense of unease. Signaling to Adrian to move closer, he reminded him of their talk earlier.

"Get out and call me." He whispered, as the Dean arrived, ending their discussion.

Assessing the situation, he rang maintenance, getting the glass replaced right away. Calling Brett over, he ordered him to keep Adrian under tighter security, at all times two guards must be with him. After reassuring Adrian that everything was okay, he left. Outside Brett pulled Milton aside.

"Maybe we should rethink leaving Adrian here."

"He stays here, that's final. Don't push it Brett or you're gone." He warned, leaving. Dan Crawford, Crammers second in command, standing with Adrian.

"He's a prick. We should get the kid away from here now." He whispered as Brett nodded, saying nothing.

Ian Johnson made ready to leave after concealing the two stranger's bodies. The day hadn't gone well he concluded. When he'd made ready to leave, after his botched attempt on the scientist, he'd spotted two men behind him. To make matters worse, they'd seen him move, opening fire. The range was too short for his rifle, so he'd drawn his pistol diving into the thick undergrowth. Moving with great care, he'd managed to remain hidden, although their constant barrage kept him from moving away from the area.

At first, he'd thought they were the University's security or FBI agents. How they'd managed to climb up here so quickly astounded him. Listening, he heard the two talking in German, as they tried to flank him. It then dawned on him that these two, like him, were here for the hundred million. Knowing the University would've called for backup by now, Ian knew he had to get away from this area and soon.

Waiting his chance, he let one of the would-be assassin's pass him, before moving further away. Loading the Barrett with two rounds he waited. The one who'd past him earlier continued searching the area that Ian had just left. Taking aim seemed like overkill to Ian as the guy was only about one hundred yards from him.

That aside, his instructors always drilled into them, that sloppiness got you killed. Training his rifle on the man, he let the man's upper torsos fill his scope sight before pulling the trigger. One second the man was standing there as the hunter. Next he was thrown to the ground becoming the prey. Positive he was dead; Ian's sense of achievement was short lived. A barrage of well-aimed shots peppered the bushes around him, one striking his left arm.

"Fuck now I'm in trouble," Ian whispered, trying to remain dead still. The second man he realised was a lot more professional than his now dead companion. Ian instincts told him to flee, his gut said to stay put. Ten minutes of lying in the undergrowth bleeding slowly to death paid off. Ian breathing softly heard the rustle of a branch being moved behind him.

Dropping the rifle, Ian again drew his pistol. Turning he fired blindly at where the sound came from. He got his first break that day, hearing a grunt of pain. This was followed by the sound of a body crashing into the undergrowth.

Moving cautiously forward he found the man lying face down shot through the head. Turning him over, he found he had a German paratrooper tattoo on his arm and short-cropped hair. Other than that there was no way of identifying him, as his face was completely gone.

"You nearly got me kraut, and that's quite an accomplishment," Ian admitted. He knew that if the guy hadn't made a noise when he'd approached him, he'd be lying dead, instead of him.

Checking his arm, he found the round had passed right through. Having no time to spare, he swiftly bandaged it, the need to get moving becoming critical. Dragging the body back to his partners, he went through their pockets finding several thousand dollars, passports and return tickets to Germany. He also found a layout of the University, and a picture of the scientist, similar to his. He surmised that the two must've either been working or holidaying in LA to get here so fast. They most probably hoped to beat other contract killers to the scientist by moving straight in.

'Might've worked if it hadn't been for me being here' he thought. Picking up one of their weapons, Ian saw it was a stub-nosed assault rifles. It wasn't a long-range weapon like his, meaning they'd planned to get up close and personal.

"They must have been moving through here to attack the rear of the University when I took the shots," He whispered, realising there might be others. Having a quick look around making sure he was alone, he loaded their money and their weapons into his pack. Covering them with his netting, he moved cautiously yet swiftly away.

Clearing the area, Ian reached his vehicle. In the distance, back towards the University, he heard the sound of the first helicopter make its first run over the area.

"Well at least I made something out of today's fiasco," he smiled, placing the two men's weapons and money in the boot of his car. Getting behind the wheel glad to be alive, Ian dropped two painkillers into his mouth trying to ease the ache in his back. Washing them down with some water from his canteen, Ian decided to stand by his golden rule. From now on he'd only work outside America.

Brett and his team left after the new window was fitted. Adrian, he found took the attempt on his life a lot better than he expected. He'd at first been a little shaky over it but had bounced back well, resuming his work. Secretly Brett hoped he took off tonight, knowing as long as he was here they'd keep coming. He decided to give him another day, if he hadn't gone by then, he'd quit and leave with him. Some things were worth quitting for.

THE ESCAPE

Realising there was too much activity for him to get away, Adrian after Brett left, returned to his unit. He stayed till dark, reading and watching the goings on outside while planning his departure. At six, with the power completely restored, he walked to the cafeteria for a light meal. His two guards came too, shadowing him. Entering he was amazed to find the place deserted. Asking one of the guards where the students all were, he told him that most had fled to town, after the Dean's speech about a student with a gun and the sniper incident.

Helping himself, he quickly consumed his meal returning to his unit. Locking the door saying goodnight to the guards, Adrian prepared to leave. He'd just finished packing his bag when he heard a noise. Walking towards the back of his unit the noise turned out to be the shower running. Putting his bag back in his closet, he silently approached the bathroom, arming himself with a knife from the kitchen.

"Who's there?" He asked peering in the door. His eyes nearly popped out, when he saw the outline of a woman showering naked through the frosted glass.

"It's me, Emma. My shower has no hot water, so I thought since I was coming to see you; I'd have a shower here." Emma's honey-sweet voice explained. "I thought with the shooting you might need some company? You don't mind do you?" she continued opening the door a faction so she could see him.

"No, it's okay." His voice quivered, as looking below her face he saw her left breast pressed up against the glass.

"Relax Adrian I won't bite you. That's unless you want me too" She giggled, her eyes watching him, as her breast stayed pushed up against the glass, driving him crazy.

"You're a beautiful woman Emma." He said softly, moving closer. This surprised her; she had thought he would run.

She'd planned this whole seduction carefully. Seeing Adrian walking back from dinner in the cafeteria, she had let herself into his apartment. Stripping quickly she had waited till she heard the door open before turning on the shower. Knowing of his experience with women, or lack of it, she had expected to be the aggressor. Emma had expected him to retreat from the bathroom after first getting him excited by her naked body.

There really was only one place he could go to, and that was his bedroom. Going to him, dressed only in a towel, she would pretend nothing had happened wanting just to discuss business. All she had to do then, was wait until the time was right and let the towel fall away. No matter how innocent or inexperienced he was, she knew he couldn't resist making love to her.

But he wasn't running. Instead he stood his ground. She thought that his near-death experience today could have caused this change, although she couldn't be sure. Emma for the first time in a long while found herself off balance. The change in him for some reason both turned her on and scared her at the same time.

Opening the shower door wide, she stood there watching him, as he slowly stripped off his clothes, his eyes never leaving hers. Naked and fully aroused, he climbed into the shower beside her. Putting his arms behind her back, he pulled her to him, kissing her full on the mouth. His hands then slid down her back kneading her flesh, before coming to rest on her arse. There they stayed, gently massaging her flesh as his kissing continued arousing her.

Without warning he suddenly gripped her arse, pulling her against him in a tight embrace. A moan escaped her lips as thrusting forward he pushed her up against the wall letting her feel his wanton need. 'Oh my God who would've thought it? He's in total control' she moaned, knowing tonight she wouldn't be faking her orgasms.

Waking as the sun came up, Emma stretched like a cat moaning softly, remembering the night. He had dominated her completely, controlling their lovemaking, pushing her to the limit. She had enjoyed every minute of it, submitting to his every command, wanting to please her new master. Just thinking of it aroused her, as she rolled over wanting more. Instead, she found an empty bed.

"Adrian," she called, thinking he was going to surprise her with breakfast. As time went by and no breakfast or Adrian appeared, she hopped out of bed, walking naked into the lounge area. Of Adrian, there was no sign. Finding the front window open, a bad feeling came over her, as retreating to the bedroom she quickly dressed. Opening the front door, she came face to face, with two security guards. Their jaws dropped, when she appeared at the door, of what they thought was an empty apartment.

"Did Adrian leave?" She asked, trying to sound in control.

"Yes, he went to his lab about twenty minutes ago. How long have you been here? The night shift didn't mention you entering?" One of the guards asked.

Slamming the door not answering, Emma went to his closet, looking inside. Last night they'd both gotten out of bed for some well-deserved drinks. She'd borrowed a shirt from this closet. While there, she'd noticed a duffel bag full of clothes on the floor. That bag was now gone. Going back to the bedroom she retrieved her shoes, finding a note. Reading it, she stood there for several seconds, before giggling uncontrollably, then laughing till she cried. Destroying the note, smiling at her night of supposed seduction, she swiftly left.

When Adrian had gone to the lab, his guards at the door ending their shift in an hour had stayed. This allowed the new crew to escort him, while they waited out their remaining time at the door. Walking to the lab, one of the new guards noticed he was carrying a bag.

"What's in the bag?" he asked.

"Bit of dry cleaning. I thought I'd drop it off on the way to lunch." Adrian answered arriving at the lab block.

Leaving him to work alone, his guards took up station outside his door. Inside, Adrian, stood near the door out of sight, listening. The guards were talking football, meaning they weren't suspicious of his bag. 'I've got to get away from here,' he told himself, moving towards the duct. Yesterday he'd consider this duct the best escape route, now he wasn't so sure.

He'd once seen it open when a new coaxial cable had been run into his lab. He's only problem with going out through the duct was its size. Locking around the room seeing no alternatives, he decided to try it and hope he didn't get trapped. Finding a screwdriver, he unscrewed the Duct panel looking inside. The entry was small, very small. Looking inside, he saw the passageway ran in two directions, widened becoming big enough to kneel in.

Fear gripped him, as the thought of getting wedged in such a tight place, gripped him. Taking several deep breaths, he decided it was better to try than to wait for another assassin. Throwing his bag in first, he got down on his hands and knees. Putting his arms through first, he squeezed his head through, then his chest. Panic seised him when he found he couldn't move forward or backwards.

Calming himself, he let the air in his lungs out, his chest constricted. Gravity did the rest, as his forward momentum pushed him down into the passageway. Waiting, making sure his fall hadn't been heard he backed down the ventalation shaft, so he could look back into his lab. Hearing no movement from the guards, he reached back inside. Moving the duct panel back in front of the opening, he secured it in place. Confident he was in the clear, he quietly wriggled his way along the passageway, following the new cable.

Twenty minutes of crawling along with aching knees, he found the cable ended. It disappeared, through a drilled hole in the wall of the duct. This worried him, as he thought the cable would lead to a service room for the network, where he could get out. Having no choice, he continued on, coming at last to another vent. Knowing he could crawl all day without finding a way out, he decided to break out here.

Kicking the vent, it broke into three large pieces, falling into the room. More confident this time, he wormed his way out into the room. Luck was with him, as it was the maintenance men's change room.

Rummaging through the lockers, he found a pair of overalls putting them on. Finding a baseball cap in another locker, he ruffled his hair placing it on his head. Looking in a mirror Adrian checked his disguise, considering it good enough to stand up to anything except a close-up inspection. Walking outside he followed the building, spotting a delivery van in one of the docks. Seeing the rear door open, he quickly stowed away in the rear behind a pile of cardboard boxes.

After ten minutes of waiting nervously, the driver returned, loading two wooden boxes before slamming the rear door. The gate he figured was his biggest chance of getting caught. The driver unaware of his stowaway would naturally stop for an inspection. Adrian worried, searched for a better spot to hide. One of the two boxes the driver had loaded contained laundry. Climbing into it, he buried himself in the clothes and waited.

The guards at the University entry gates weren't too worried about people leaving, only entering. After a brief look inside, the van was waved through. The next problem he thought about was getting out. Climbing out of the laundry box, Adrian went to the side of the truck, finding it had a door there. Pulling the handle quietly he found it opened, so he closed it again and waited. After an hour of sitting in the dark, he felt the truck slow down. Cracking the door again, he saw they were stopped at a set of lights.

"Now or never," He grimaced, as opening the door he jumped out, closing it behind him. He heard the driver shout behind him, but he was long gone before he managed to get out and give chase Running down several alleys just to be sure, Adrian feeling he'd made it, slowed down emerging onto a busy sidewalk. Blending in with the people out shopping he wandered down the street looking at several shops before boarding a bus for the city centre.

"Well that was easy" he smiled. "Now it's time for the second part of my plan."

Twenty minutes after Adrian had left; four men entered the campus over a rear fence. Breaking into two groups, they walked casually towards Adrian's lab. Power had been restored the night before to the surveillance cameras and the computer facility, so the Security staff on duty weren't taken by surprise. As the Campus was near deserted, facial ID quickly showed the staff that the men weren't students or employees.

Calling Brett they told him their direction, tipping off all patrolling units about their presence. Wanting as little bloodshed as possible, Brett had a group of ten agents waiting at the Lab. As the four men approached the building, they all donned ski masks, showing how little they knew of the security. Pulling out an odd collection of firearms they entered the lobby.

Here they found a room full of armed agents pointing their weapons straight at them.

"I suggest lowering your weapons onto the floor," Brett ordered them, as the four men, taken aback, dropped them guns immediately. Going forward the men were frisked and handcuffed, before being bundled outside to wait for the local police. It seemed they were from LA. Having heard of the reward they had decided to have a go themselves.

"Bloody amateurs!" One agent barked, standing watch over them, as the others laughed.

"I rather these clowns than the other type." Brett pointed out, sobering his men.

Most of the men there had been at the Uni the day before when the sniper took his shots. They knew that man was still out there after they'd found two men shot dead on the hill. Ballistics had confirmed that one man had been killed with the same weapon, fired at Adrian. Why the two had been killed remained a mystery. Both were ex-army from Germany, other than that, they were nobodies.

The FBI suspected they were freelarce hit men, but nothing else solid. Watching the four men being led away, Brett worried, asked for an update on Adrian. It didn't take long for his guards to report him gone. Brett outwardly cursed the guards inwardly he felt relieved.

Dean Campbell went ballistic when news reached him that Adrian had vanished. Several times he tried to contact Emma, wanting to know what she'd done that night. For some reason, she'd turned off her phone. The guards at the gate reported they'd seen her leave the campus, since then nothing.

"Send her an email and a recorded message on her phone. Tell her, that she is fired!" Milton exploded. Looking for any more decent, he turned on the FBI officers in the room. "Where the fucks Darren Cramer? This mess is his fault!"

"His car was reported entering Canada. Since then we've failed to contact him." Dan Crawford, the senior FBI agent, there replied, standing his ground.

"Where's Brett then? He at least I still trust."

"He's out looking for Adrian, and weren't you going to fire him the other day?" Dan answered sarcastically, a small smile on his lips.

"You watch your mouth, I give the orders here."

"We already have a boss, his name is Director Douglas. And if I remember rightly, yesterday you were advised by both Brett and Darren to move Adrian Hayes, but refused. I'm sure our boss will be real happy to hear that." Dan smiled. Dean Campbell, turning red, moved up to stand toe to toe with Crawford; he was about to put him in his place when his phone rang.

"Who is it?" Milton screeched into the phone.

"The President." Came an angry response, as Dean Campbell's face, went white.

"I'm sorry Mr President I didn't know it was you." Milton stammered out.

"Obviously, now, how are things going? The CIA told me there's been a leak there. It hasn't affected the research has it?" The President asked, as the Dean vomiting, dropped his phone.

Brett the next morning received a brief text message from Adrian. It told him he had left the campus and was staying under an assumed name at the hotel close to the one they stayed at on their hunting trips. To check it was really him, Brett sent a return message, saying he'd heard Adrian had company last night. The return message said, 'she'd eat him for breakfast'. Brett smiling remembered the first time Adrian had asked for Emma's number.

Knowing it was him, Brett being careful, asked him to meet him that night at 7 at their favourite bar. Getting, 'I hope Linda's serving' as a reply, made Brett start planning. Ringing Dan and telling him he'd located Adrian, he asked for an additional three agents to help pick him up. Arranging a safe house for them to secure him in, he was told by Dan about their trouble with the Dean and the President calling.

They now had the Dean under house arrest. The President was none too happy with what had transpired; he'd ordered every government agency to prioritise' their activities, putting the finding of Adrian Hayes at the top.

He also wanted everyone working for the drug cartels, to be taken care of, one way or the other.

At the moment the CIA was having a field day arresting over seventy wanted fugitives entering the country. The thought of that enormous bounty was bringing many hard-line killers into the open where they were vulnerable. Homeland security and the FBI were also having significant successes. Between them, prisons were overflowing with the drug industry's best hitmen, caught either entering California or at the LA airport.

From Brett's point of view, he knew it took only one professional to get through to kill Adrian. The University's security and the outside units couldn't plug every leak, already some like the four today would've made it into the area. That's why it was so essential to secure Adrian. Once the opposition knew he was safe, they'd stop coming.

Looking at his watch, he saw it as nearing 10 in the morning, which gave him till 9hrs till he met Adrian. Deciding to return to the University to prepare, Brett wondered what had happened to Darren.

VANCOUVER

Darren gazed out over Vancouver's harbour precinct. It was going to be a perfect day for the people who lived and worked here he mused. Across from where he sat, the cruise ship terminal was busy. On either side of the terminal sat two massive Dutch-owned ships. They were preparing for their trips up into Alaska, to see the glaciers and the pristine coastal scenery. As if on cue, a seaplane took off opposite the cruise ships, the tourists on board both ships, rushing to the side of the vessels to watch it.

He spent the day before driving like a maniac, to catch up with Loraine, only to find she'd crossed into Canada. Reaching the border near Seattle, half-deranged with anger, he wanted an explanation, as to why she had been allowed to cross. A surprised border guard had told him bluntly, that the alert had been issued after she had already crossed.

Calming down, apologising, he'd thanked the guards, before driving over the border continuing on. He kept following the cars Sat Nav for the rest of the day, in the end coming upon the car abandoned in a backstreet suburb of Vancouver. Spending the entire night showing a photo he had of her, to hotel staff throughout Vancouver had paid off.

Figuring with her newfound wealth, she'd be staying somewhere flashy, he'd targeted the best hotels. At the Vancouver Hyatt, he hit paid dirt, finding a staff member who'd seen her enter that evening as he came on shift. Not being able to show his badge, he staked out the hotel waiting.

Nine in the morning she had left the hotel looking a million dollars. Making sure her bags were loaded onto a small shuttle, she had walked towards the cruise terminal. Obviously she'd booked a trip while she planned the rest of her life, he'd concluded. So now he sat on his bench by the harbourside, wondering if he had guts to confront her. Getting up, he quickly checked his weapon. Cocking it, he walked boldly towards the cruise ships terminal.

Loraine had made one big mistake. Although ships left Vancouver for cruises to Alaska, all passengers had to pass through US customs, before boarding. He knew this wouldn't worry her greatly, because by now she was using an alias. The mistake was, he now had jurisdiction, as the terminal was considered US territory.

Showing his badge he passed through American customs. Explaining the situation, he gave the description of a woman, who was travelling on her own. It didn't take long; most of the guards remembered the hot little number who flirted with them, before boarding. Getting her room number, he went aboard, having been warned the ship sailed in four hours. She was booked into one of the exclusive suites on the top deck, making finding her easy.

Approaching the cabin, he intercepted a steward who was just leaving her room. Showing his badge he had the man reopen the cabin door, indicating for him to leave. Seeing Darren pull out his gun, he swiftly fled. Entering the room, he checked the suite, finding the bathroom door locked. Approaching the door he stood listening, hearing Loraine humming happily in the shower.

Tears welled up in his eyes he knew that despite all that had happened, he still loved her. Pulling out his keys, he used one to turn the latch opening the door. She had her back to him, as she stood naked under the shower. Putting away his gun Darren tapped on the wall making her swing around covering herself. Both of them stood frozen, their eyes locked on one another, unable to talk.

"I'm so sorry Darren." She whimpered covering herself with a towel, as Darren crying collapsed onto the floor. Moving to him she hugged him sobbing with him.

"I've got to take you back." He whispered holding her, trying to wipe the tears from his eyes.

"I know. For what it's worth, I'm sorry for what I did to you, Darren. I really do love you; I just wanted to have some money."

"You'd better get dressed." He said pushing her away and standing up. Drying herself, she moved past him to the bed where she'd laid out her clothes. Standing beside her, he watched her put on her bra and underwear. Looking at him, unable to stand it any longer, she rushed into his arms.

"Forgive me, Darren, I don't want to leave here knowing you hate me?" She sobbed.

"I don't hate you, Loraine." He replied pulling her head up and kissing her. Before he could stop himself, he'd ripped off her underwear, pushing her back onto the bed. It was the most intense lovemaking they had ever had, as each tried to enjoy this last fleeting moment in time before they left each other forever. Both came at the same time, crying out in exhilaration and in anguish, hugging each their lovers. Finished, unable to look at each other, they both silently dressed.

Darren knew the customs men would be waiting for him and his prisoner, so they'd have to leave the ship. He hadn't told her, but once they'd passed through customs, he was going to let her go. He couldn't stand the thought of the woman he loved going to prison. Instead, he decided to wear the consequences. Approaching the cabin door, Darren carrying her bag, saw the door handle start to move. Thinking it was the police trying the door, he was surprised when two masked men burst in.

Felix like his boss didn't like loose ends. Sending another message to his two men, he told them to make sure she didn't talk after retrieving the file. It hadn't taken them long to track her to Vancouver. Every time she used the fake credit cards they'd given her, the bank would tell Felix the cards position, which he passed on. They too had waited outside the hotel. Unable to get close to her as she left the hotel, they'd boarded the cruise ship, posing as crewmembers. The last thing they were expecting was to meet an armed agent.

As they forced the door, they came face to face with the target and a man about to leave. Both cartel men went for their guns, as the man with Loraine, threw her bag at them slamming the door.

Off balance by the thrown suitcase the men opened fire spraying the door, as Darren on his side, fired through the door as well. Although both men were hit in the exchange, they still charged the door, trying to finish the job. The door wouldn't give, so both them pushed harder.

Behind them, three Customs officers, who had been sent by the local police to arrest Darren were just entering the corridor to Loraine's room. Director Douglas having been informed of Loraine's treachery and Darren's disappearance had asked the Vancouver police to detain both of them. Hearing the shots, they drew their weapons.

Rounding a corner, they spotted the two men, still trying to enter the suite. Calling for them both to drop their weapons, the men momentarily surprised, turned towards the new threat, opening fire. Both of Felix's men went down, repeatedly shot by the taken aback officers.

Cautiously moving forward, the officers checked the shooters, finding them both dead. Putting their shoulders to the door, they opened it to find both Loraine and Darren face down on the floor behind it. Checking them both, they found the woman dead, although Darren was still breathing. Calling in a downed officer code, they rushed Darren to the deck. There they were met by an approaching Medical Evac helicopter.

As it swooped down onto the deck, Darren was swiftly transferred aboard. The chopper captain, getting the all clear immediately took off, heading for a nearby hospital, as the tourist on board clamoured for photos. The crew on board the chopper, worked frantically to stabilise Darren, as looking over the harbour the pilot saw the hospital come into sight.

"You'll be okay buddy we're nearly there, just hang on!" The Captain yelled as the crewmembers assured him he'd be okay, trying to urge him on.

"You know, it really is a perfect day." Darren murmured smiling, before dying.

THE FIASCO

Brett sat at the bar his mouth tasting like ash. He thought he'd feel better with Loraine's death. Instead he felt a great sadness for a man he'd misjudged. News of the shootout aboard the cruise ship had made headlines around the world. The news networks put it down to a failed robbery, which a brave FBI agent had tried to prevent. The exact details weren't being released, but it didn't stop the media from guessing.

Fear started to grip Brett as he waited for Adrian to surface. Things were going downhill rapidly. Serious hitters were looking for him; it was only a matter of time until they located him.

"For fuck sake where are you?" Brett said out loud, making several patrons turn towards him. One glare, made them look away.

"Take it easy Brett, everything will be alright." Linda's voice sounded from behind him.

When they'd arrived at the bar, Brett had come clean and briefed Linda on what was happening, not why. She had willingly helped them, watching for anyone out of the ordinary. He'd brought three agents with him; two watched the front door, while Dan, formerly Darren second in command watched the rear. Since the episode at the University with the gunmen, Brett had come to the conclusion that he could be trusted. What worried him was Adrian was late. It wasn't like him.

"Any sign of Adrian." Brett barked into his Comm's gear. He received no's from the three agents, all seem on edge. The place was packed to the rafters, way too crowded to watch everywhere at once.

"There he is!" Linda yelled pointing at the dance floor. Brett jumped to his feet moving forward. He saw Adrian wave to him, then disappear, as another man appeared right behind him. Whatever the guy said to Adrian made him look towards Brett, before he lost sight of him. In the seething mass, he could be anywhere? Switching on his transmitter, he alerted the others that Adrian was here, getting an okay from the two front door agents. When he heard no reply from Dan at the rear, he called again. Still getting no answer, Brett nervous tried to locate Adrian in the crowd.

"Someone's got, Adrian!" Linda screamed as Brett drawing his weapon surged into the crowd. Yelling to his men to head towards the rear door, he saw a man with a moustache and long brown hair leading Adrian at gunpoint outside. Reaching the door, Brett found Dan lying on the ground unconscious. Leaving him, he raced after Adrian, through a sea of stunned faces.

Rounding a corner, he saw Adrian being pushed into a dark van as the longhaired man turned. He was holding, what looked like a Mac10 submachine gun. Seeing Brett he smiled, pulling the trigger. For a little gun, it sounded like the end of the world, as Brett and the two other agents who had arrived, joined him diving for cover.

The guy let go a full clip, before jumping into the van, which instantly accelerated away. Gaining his feet, Brett took aim, as the van screeched around a corner disappearing. Chaos descended on the street behind them, as the club goers stampeded away from the roar of the gun.

"Fuck no!" Brett cursed, screaming out his frustration, as the other agents came up beside him. Calling the local cops, Brett issued a description of the van, knowing it was all he could do. Moving back to the rear door they found Linda, looking after the downed agent. Brett looked around surprised. He expected to have people down everywhere, including himself, from the shots fired.

"Where'd the bullets go?" One of the agents asked as Brett tried to work out what was going on. Linda helping Dan to his feet, held him as the two other agents took an arm each, moving him back inside. Free of his care, Linda ran to Brett.

"Will they hurt him?" Linda asked. Brett lost for words, at first couldn't answer.

"He'll be okay. Whoever took him wanted him alive. Don't worry." Brett assured her. Inside he felt gutted, at his friend's loss.

After a search of the area found zero, Brett went to the FBI's headquarters in LA. As he expected he didn't receive a warm welcome. Questions were being asked about the whole security at the University and the club stakeout. With Dean Campbell under house arrest and Darren dead, the mess fell into Brett's lap. Arriving on the tenth floor of the Federal building, he was escorted to the supervisor's office.

"This mess is your fault. You and your ex-partner Crammer from New York are a disgrace. If he weren't dead already, he'd be in prison." Sharn Davison, the LA supervisor, screamed at Brett, who'd only just entered her office. At any other time, Brett would've thought Sharn was an attractive woman, but not now.

"Wouldn't you like to hear my report on what happened, before you blame me for everything?" Brett answered, trying to get over her attitude and get something moving.

"What's the point? You're a burnt out mindless agent just as corrupt as your ex-partner Crammer." With that reply, Brett exploded.

"I didn't screw my way to the top like you did Miss Davison. And if you talk about Darren like that again, I'll break your fucking jaw!" He snarled, watching her move back.

"You can consider yourself fired you drunken bum, get out!" She screamed, as Brett knowing his career was over, gave her the finger.

"Go` screw yourself. It will be a change for you." He laughed turning and slamming her glass door. The impact with the door frame shattered it, spraying the supervisor's room with glass. "You can take that out of my severance pay," Brett yelled back, not turning around. In the central area were at least twenty agents, standing pretending to work, while listening. Some smiled, others turned away, trying to stop from laughing. Brett, his head held high, walked towards the lift.

Riding the lift down, Brett cursed his stupidity. He'd kissed his career goodbye, but more importantly, he'd lost his chance to help Adrian. Depressed he decided on a drink to deaden the pain.

Sharn Davison sat at her office desk watching one of their cleaners; scoop up another handful of glass from the floor.

"How can I further destroy that bastard?" She snarled out loud, making the cleaner swiftly shovel another load of glass into his bucket, before swiftly leaving. He had shamed her in front of her minions, humiliating her. Sharn wanted more than revenge, she wanted him to crawl back here and beg for her forgiveness. "I'll blacken his name so no one will hire him. He'll have to come back here then" She mused, smiling, as her phone started to ring.

"What now?" She cursed picking it up. "Who is it?"

"It's the man holding Adrian Hayes so shut up and listen." A voice commanded as Sharn jumping to her feet had one of her men run a trace on the call.

"Go ahead I'm listening." She replied. After staying quiet for two minutes she dropped the phone, glaring at it.

"Did you trace the call?" She screamed getting a head shake indicating no.

"Shit! Shit! Shit!" She screamed, calling Director Douglas.

Brett was just leaving the FBI building, when two guards from the foyer ran after him, blocking his path. 'Shit what now' he thought, wondering if that bitch Davison was going to have him arrested

"You're wanted back upstairs." The guard advised him, though he could see they wouldn't let him pass. Nodding his thanks, slightly confused, Brett rode the lift back up. Alighting again in the main area, he prepared himself for what was coming. Supervisor Davison was waiting at the lift with two agents for him. Silence settled over the entire room as they all waited to see what happened. In the end Supervisor, Davison broke the silence.

"The man supposedly holding Adrian Hayes just called. He refused to negotiate with anyone but you. Why is that do you think?"

"No idea. Maybe he's from New York and knows me from a bar I get wasted in." Brett replied smiling, before becoming serious. "Did you trace the call?"

Sharn Davison stood staring as if he was shit on her new shoes. In the end, she caved him.

"No, he didn't stay on the line long enough."

"Did you get anything else?" Brett asked. Sharn knowing she had no choice, moved on.

"Against my advice, Director Douglas has put you in charge of the negotiating. I'm to give you every assistance, in getting Adrian Hayes back safely. The kidnapper said he'd call back in three hours. I suggest since you're such a hotshot agent, you listen to the tape of the conversation yourself." Sharn told him as if chewing sand, before turning and starting to walk back to her office.

"That's great, later we'll have coffee maybe at your place?" Brett yelled after her, making her miss a step. Clenching her fist, she continued to her office, slamming the door. What was left of the glass from Brett's earlier altercation, crashed to the floor in response.

With the supervisor's exit, suppressed laughter broke out amongst the gathered agents. Picking the 3 men, plus the agents from the stakeout at the club, including Dan, Brett asked if there was a room set up for kidnappings. He was told on floor nine below them, the FBI had a situation room for special circumstances like this. Asking them to draft who they thought they'd need, he headed down.

The room resembled the room they used in New York for the same situations. It was large enough for at least twenty agents and their staff to work comfortably in while keeping in contact with the field teams. To the left side of the door as you entered, was the communications area, containing phones and radios. The opposite side to the right of the door was a group of large whiteboards, for photos and information.

Next to them was a huge TV screen and an area for conferences. The far wall was made up of banks of desks and of course a coffee machine. The middle was where

Brett would be, the heart and brains of the operation. From here all decision flowed out to the rest of the room, he hoped he was up to it.

As the kidnapper had promised, he rang back in 3 hours. Brett in the meantime had gone over the tape of the conversation. The only thing he got of it was the guy had an accent.

"Is that Agent Heckle?"

"Yes, whom am I talking to?"

"They call me The Cuban. To you, I'm the man who's got, Adrian Hayes." Brett listened carefully to the guy's accent this time. He surmised that it was Spanish.

"How do we know he's alive?"

"Ask a question."

"I'd rather hear his voice."

"Well you can't, so ask a question!"

"I'm hanging up unless I hear his voice." Brett threatened. Around him, he saw agents opened mouth at him threatening to hang up on their only lead.

"Look arsehole, he's being held somewhere else. So ask a question, and I'll reroute it to him." Brett pondered if his accent had slipped slightly.

"How much does he owe me?" Brett asked as the agents around him looked on confused. Silence answered Brett question, as he waited. A faint sound of people talking could be heard on the phone from the kidnapper's end.

"He's said ten percent if that means something." The Cuban replied sounding baffled. Brett relieved continued.

"Okay, I believe you, what do you want?"

"Money of course and lot's of it."

"How much?"

"The same as the syndicate is paying, a hundred million US dollars."

"That's a shit load of money my friend. I've got a question for you. If the syndicates are offering you that much, why are you coming to us?"

"Adrian tells me his discovery can be used as a weapon of unimaginable power. Somehow I trust America with it, more than a group of drug suppliers."

"I'll have to ask my boss, but like I said, that's a lot of money."

"So are millions of people starving to death? I'll ring in two days. You'd better have the right answer." The kidnapper pointed out, hanging up.

Turning to an agent who was running a trace he indicated they had the address. Ten minutes of frantic calling had a local police swat team there. All they found, was an abandoned building with a phone line, even the phone was gone. Back at the office, they had their crimes department go over the tape of the kidnappers call.

"The guy is about twenty years old, and he speaks with a Spanish accent. The accent could be put on to hide his real nationality, but we're not sure. We checked records, and there are several reports of an assassin going by the name of 'The Cuban'. The accent and age fit his descriptions, but it could be a copycat for all we know. Also, when you were waiting for an answer to your question, he was whispering to someone in the background in Spanish. So like at the club, there are at least two of them involved."

"Good work people, it's not much to go on, but at least Adrian Hayes is safe," Brett told them. "Now let's see if the Government wants to pay?" He smiled. Inside he felt like throwing up. He knew they had nothing.

THE WHITEHOUSE

The President was far from happy when he was told about the money required for Adrian's release.

"Goddammit, he's not even a voting American. We're not going to be blackmailed into paying them a dime. There will be no negotiating with them."

"What about his research Sir?" Senator Jeffries asked.

"We've got his data recorded, we don't need him." The President pointed out.

"No, we haven't Sir. When he disappeared we checked his data, it would appear someone introduced a virus into his research notes during the transfer. It's all gone." The President was speechless for several seconds before he replied.

"This is inexcusable I want whoever responsible found!" He roared.

"It's being looked into Sir, but what about Hayes?"

"What are they asking?"

"One hundred million."

"That's a lot of money Senator. Shit, we could build a City Hospital with that kind of money." The President pointed out, thinking. "Can we get it from somewhere, off the books?"

"Yes, Sir. When we set this Think-tank program up over forty years ago, we started retaining the patents of scientists and researchers like Adrian Hayes. We've built up billions in investments, which is how we fund our University's projects. We could take the money from there. It would hurt future funding, but we can live with it."

"Go ahead then. Make it clear that I want this blackmailer apprehended and the money returned." The President ordered, none too happy.

"No problem Sir. I'll notify treasury about the money transfer. They have the means to trace it." Jeffries smiled.

"I don't know what I do without you Daniel. You've proved a trusted friend." The President confessed.

"Thank you, Sir. I'm just glad to be able to help." He smiled leaving.

When Jeffries had cleared the Whitehouse, he had his chauffer take him to his office. The Senator's seat was from California, but like most politicians, he kept an office in Washington where he could work in private. Having his two bodyguards wait outside, he went into his inner office closing the door. Here he had a direct hardwired computer terminal connecting him to his Swiss bank. Totally secure needing an authorisation code and a thumbprint he connected with his account.

For over twenty years Jeffries had as President of the company successfully run the Think Tank University program for the Government. What they didn't know, was he had over those years, syphoned off a large number of patents and more importantly money from the accounts. Through careful management and investments, it now rivalled the money under the control of the government.

The problem at the moment was that all the funds in the government accounts were tied up providing resources for running the Think tanks. He could move some of those assets from the accounts, but someone might notice how short they were at the moment. This was due to his skimming of another one hundred million from the account earlier that very month.

Undoing his creative bookwork, he transferred the funds back to the government accounts before transferring it to an account the FBI could use for the exchange. Checking his account he saw over 1.7 Billion worth of shares and cash sitting happily waiting for his retirement in three years. He couldn't help chuckling at the size of the funds he had amassed while receiving accolades from the government for his tireless service to his country.

Thinking about Adrian's project, his smile faltered, as he thought of the countless Billions this discovery would produce. He knew greed had always been his weakness, but it was so easy.

He'd started off as a Dean of one of the Government's original Think tank University's. His job back then was to make sure that patents remained in the Universities name. He'd been working away for about two years when an idea came to him. It occurred to him that the Government had no way of tracking which patents were theirs and which were the actual inventors or scientists.

He'd decided as a test, to transfer some into his own name. To his surprise no one did anything. He noticed that as long as the flow of money to the Government-owned accounts continued to grow, no one cared less. For several years he slowly built up a sizable fortune, getting more aggressive in' his stealing. Unfortunately, while he was in the process of changing over several patents from one incredible successful scientist, he came undone.

The man out of the blue asked to see his patents. The scientist named Andrew had decided without warning to retire early. This had completely surprised him. At first, he'd tried to bluff Andrew into thinking the University held all his patents because he worked for them. It hadn't worked. The scientist demanded the authorities be brought in to investigate it.

Pacifying him, Jeffries suggested a board meeting to discuss it, that night. Andrew confident readily agreed, this gave Jeffries time to plan. When the time of the board meeting arrived later that night, he angrily told Andrew that the board members weren't coming, that he was being fired instead. Ordering him off the University's grounds, Jeffries then raced to his car and waited.

The scientist in the meantime was furious, threatening legal actions. The guards who were ordered to escort him off the premises found his aggressive behaviour strange, to say the least. Later this aggression would help explain the accident, as Jeffries hinted that Andrew had been drinking at work, causing him to have him escorted from the University grounds.

Following him, Jeffries waited for just the right spot before running the distracted man off the road. Stopping seeing he was dead, Jeffries at first was shocked by what he'd done. Vomiting on the side of the road Jeffries stood shaking guilt-ridden by his callous murdering of an innocent man. As time passed, he realised that with the man, he could now take all of his patents, not just a few as he had intended. Returning to the University, he spent the night forging all Andrew's patents. By the next day, he doubted even Andrew would've been able to prove anything.

Andrew's wife had been suspicious, but without proof, she could do nothing. Jeffries had by using contacts inside the Government, got her terminated from the power plant where she worked. This cut off her financial support, isolating her, although she still managed to hire a nosey Detective. The grubby little man to Jeffries' surprise, found a link from the patents of other scientists back to him. This had again forced him to take care of the problem detective, and unlike before, he'd had no qualms about killing the man.

Since then he'd managed to steer clear of any more problems by being more careful with his paperwork. Tying the scientists in knots with legal jargon was far easier and financially more rewarding than the alternative of getting rid of them.

Smiling thinking how smart he'd been, he closed down his terminal. Making sure the accounts were again secure, he made ready to leave. Looking at his watch, he saw he had less than two hours to reach the airport for his flight to New York. There he intended to look at some Real estate property, to add to his property portfolio. Turning he had just reached the door when behind him, he heard his computer beep twice.

Suspicious, he returned to the computer terminal. Checking it, he made sure it was turned off. He'd never heard those beeps before, and when so much hung on the security of his assets, anything out of the ordinary bothered him. Starting up the terminal again, he had the security system checked to make sure it was functioning perfectly. Showing no faults, he shut it down again watching as the console after checking its own integrity, switched off. This time it didn't beep.

Putting it down to nerves Jeffries left his office, making a mental note to have the whole installation serviced and scanned.

THE DEMONS

News that the government was willing to pay took Brett by surprise. The Government had a firm policy of not negotiating with terrorists or blackmailers. That was until of course it was revealed that the data had been erased. This explained their hasty consent and caring attitude he surmised.

Over the past two days, Brett had moved Heaven and Earth to get something going on the kidnappers. A painstaking search of surrounding traffic cameras had given them a brief description of the two suspects and the license plates of the van leaving Linda's club. By following its progress they narrowed down the search area, finding the van abandoned and burnt out in an industrial park. No DNA or prints were found on the van, and it had been reported stolen a week earlier. The other search was about the Cuban's shooting spree.

Though a thorough search was carried out no bullets, were found, only casings. Forensics came to the conclusion that the guy with the moustache had been using blanks. Why would a kidnapper, a trained assassin, use blanks? It wasn't as if he'd be worried about collateral damage, so why go to the trouble of sparing peoples lives? Brett personally believed the guy was an amateur, using this Cubans identity to disguise his own.

Still, even if he was inexperienced, it didn't explain not wanting innocent people hurt. It would've been far better to kill the FBI agents present and a few bystanders, it would've shown he meant business. Having no other leads, Brett waited for the kidnapper to again ring, hoping to get something from the next call and a better feel for this so-called Cuban assassin.

Unlike last time, when they'd talked, this time they received an SMS message, which contained a picture of Adrian holding the morning's paper. It also had the details on an exchange, giving a numbered bank account where the money would be wired too before they released Adrian. Details of where the exchange was to take place and the drop off time were also supplied. Unhappy, but with no choice, Brett sent a return message agreeing, explaining the money had been authorised in exchange for Adrian.

The Cuban cheekily replied, thanking him for his help, promising to contact him the day before the exchange. Brett had in rage smashed the laptop. Looking around, Brett didn't have to ask anyone in the Situation room how it was going. His small group had grown to fill the whole room, and that didn't include the field agents and swat teams out in the field. Their job was to follow up any leads that came in, no matter how feeble they were. Depressed needing a drink badly, Brett looked up from his desk to see Supervisor Sharn watching him from the door. Smugly she walked in, as the room grew still.

"How's the investigation going Agent Heckle?" She asked trying to hide her obvious joy at his coming failure.

"As good as could be expected under the circumstances."

"You're chewing up a lot of this office's resources in manpower and money. It would better be worth it?"

"The President seems to think so." Brett reminded her.

"Yes, I've seen the brief on the amount of money being paid. You want to hope everything goes okay."

"I'll be happy if we get Adrian back. That's all I care about at the moment." Brett answered, his patience getting thin.

"It's going to be fun watching you fall." She whispered smiling, before leaving. Brett had no answer as she walked away.

An hour after Sharn left, the photo of Adrian had been analysed. It didn't help either. Although Adrian appeared in good health considering, the medical expert examining the photo was worried. He pointed out that Adrian's irises were unusually large. This meant he was most probably heavily drugged. Brett nearly broke then, feeling he'd failed his friend.

After the Supervisor's visit, the room had thinned markedly, as agents sensing the coming failure, left the sinking ship. Calling a meeting of who was left, Brett asked if anyone had something to get the operation moving. A wall of 'I've got nothing' stared back at him. Defeated Brett decided to go over the handover plan. Cutting his loses, he came to a conclusion, that he'd be happy to just get Adrian back in one piece.

He knew to get these bastards, he had to get at least one of these kidnappers, at the handover. The money he knew was gone. Once they transferred it, they'd never see it again. So bagging the people dropping Adrian off was their main chance of salvaging something, other than Adrian. At least thirty men would cover the exchange. It was a downtown location, on the corner of a busy intersection. Snipers would cover every approach, while backup cars waited just out of sight, to close down the entire area for a block in every direction.

He was just explaining the operation for a second time when he felt a stirring move through his team. Looking behind him towards the door, he saw two men in well-tailored black business suits, standing there watching them.

"Fucking spooks!" Someone whispered next to him, as the group began talking softly amongst themselves. Calling a break, Brett excused himself.

As he walked over towards the two men, he saw the younger man's mouth say 'that's him' to the older one. He knew then that these two vultures were here to talk with him.

"My names Agent Brett Heckle, can I help you?" He asked as the two men stood looking at him as if expecting him to bow down. 'Fuck this is going to cost me' Brett thought, waiting for one of them to say something. The older of the two flourished a badge, followed by his obvious junior. As one of his team had declared earlier, they were fucking spooks from Langley.

Special Agent's Brown and Smith had come to make him aware of some information, which had come into their possession. After that both men remained silent, both waiting for him to beg. They knew he'd hit a dead end in the investigation, so he guessed they had something big. The problem for Brett was how much of his soul they wanted from him.

"Gentlemen if you have something that could help us solve this case it's in the country's best interest if you tell me." Brett reminded them, seeing a slight grin appeared on both their faces at his 'showing of the flag,' appealing to their patriotism.

"Problem is Brett. We can call you Brett can't we?" Agent Brown smiled, Brett nodding his consent, nearly choking on his capitulation to these two scumbags. "It's just the CIA is forbidden from operating inside our borders. You understand don't you?" Brown grinned, reeling him in. Brett visualised reaching across and pistol-whipping the cocksucker, before putting the boot into his fucking worthless head. Instead, he sold his soul.

"Look I know how it is if there's anything I can do to help you in return, consider it done." Brett heard himself say, the words tasting like shit in his mouth.

"We knew we could count on you." Brown smiled, as Agent Smith dropped a small USB stick into his hand. "We'll be in touch." Brown sneered looking him in the eye, assuring him his soul was gone. They both then at the same time turned, sliding back into the darkness of the hallway outside the door, vanishing he surmised through a crack in the floor.

"Returning to hell with what little of a soul I still possessed.'" He whispered as if Satan himself was listening. Brett stood staring after them for several seconds, fingering the USB stick. The silence behind him, made him turn around. The whole room stood watching him, before abruptly looking elsewhere. 'Shit they all know I've sold my soul. Probably think I'm going to suck the blood out of their children' he smiled. Realising he was over-dramatizing what had happened, he moved to his desk, loading the stick onto his laptop.

Looking over the information, he connected his laptop to the big screen on the wall located near the whiteboards so everyone could look. It showed three distinct groups of men. Putting the first group up showing a background of the hills above LA, he heard a gasp from behind him.

"Who is it?" He asked the agent.

"That's Son Tang. He heads up the Golden Triangle Asian drug cartel. What the hell is he doing here?" The Agent exclaimed. Not answering Brett flicked to the next group of men.

"I'm not completely sure of his name, but I think that guy in the photo is an Islamic militant who runs the drug trade in Afghanistan and Pakistan." Another agent pointed out.

"Mohamed Jamal is his name," Brett answered having been briefed once about him. "Does anyone know the remaining group?" He asked as the third group of men appeared on the screen. Silence followed until Dan suggested they looked like they were from South America, maybe from Nicaragua or Argentina.

"Well, gentlemen whoever the third group is, they are most certainly in the drug trade, like the other two groups and all in LA. Our spooky friends pointed out a connection with these three groups and our kidnapped scientist. Let's get to it men, we've got a week until the handover, so let's break something loose." He ordered as his team reinvigorated, raced to their phones.

"What did it cost you?" Dan asked softly from behind him, startling Brett.

"Nothing yet, but I promised to help them out in the future."

"You might be lucky. They might just bend you over, and butt fuck you." Dan sniggered, making Brett laugh.

ALLIES

Supervisor Sharn Davison viewed the CIA intervention with growing unease. One of her men on Brett's team had tipped her off, about the new information. She'd been looking forward to gutting Agent Heckle after his remark about sleeping her way to the top. True that's what she'd done, though at the time it had been necessary.

By rights, the job should have been hers years ago, but she had tits which meant she wasn't in the men's club that controlled the FBI. So having no other choice, she'd used her body to advance her career. Where brains had got her nowhere, her tight arse and good figure had opened doors. Maybe bedroom doors, but doors just the same and she had no intention of giving up the position she had earned.

Examining Brett's file, she knew that he'd been shafted by Crammer and had been a gifted agent. The problem was if he succeeded without her, he might be given her position here as a reward. Looking at the Intel he had on the three Cartels she saw a chance for her to climb right to the top, taking the Directors position. There'd been rumours the Director was retiring next year and the President she knew, was looking for someone new for the position.

He'd been an advocate for introducing females into top positions in Government, why not the FBI? Swallowing her pride, hoping it was all she'd have to swallow, she asked Brett to meet her for dinner at her apartment that night, to discuss the operation.

Brett to say the least was surprised by the invitation. Guessing the reason, he at first considered backing off, pointing out he was too busy. In the end, hoping to get more manpower, he agreed, though he remained guarded. Arriving at her apartment overlooking the ocean he was impressed. He heard rumours that Sharn was from a wealthy family, now he knew the truth.

Having had a mile of paperwork to do before this meeting, Brett had showered at work, coming straight to her apartment. He'd considered stopping for a drink on the way to steady his nerves, but had decided against it, worried she could fire him for being back on the booze. Parking his car, Brett walked to the foyer, pressing her unit button finding it to be the penthouse. A few seconds wait found her voice happily telling him to enter the lift.

The building was completely automated, controlled by the tenants. Each floor was a separate unit, and the only way to enter was to be the owner with an access code, or be like he was now, being given permission to enter by Sharn. Riding the lift up, Brett stared at the camera, wondering if she was studying him becoming edgy.

Alighting from the lift, Brett found himself standing in a large lounge area. One side was the kitchen, the other a hallway heading off to bedrooms he presumed. What he couldn't help staring at in awe, was the view of the Pacific out the full-length windows in front of him. Walking mesmerised to the windows, he opened the door walking out onto the deck.

"It's quite impressive isn't it?" A female voice said, from the side of the balcony. Looking to his right Brett found Sharn, relaxing on a leather chair looking out over the water. Unlike at work where she wore a simple business like suit, here she had on a simple black dress, with a split up the side to her thighs allowing free movement. It wasn't by any means the dress of a seductress who was trying to entice him. Although it did accentuate her incredible figure, something Brett found attractive.

"I judge you didn't get this with FBI pay?"

"No family money I'm afraid.

"Still it's a beautiful place to live, no matter who paid for it," Brett admitted sitting down. "So boss, what do you want from me?"

"After your remarks the other day I wanted to destroy you. Unfortunately, you seemed to have found some serious help, so I'm covering myself and assisting you." Sharn confessed, watching his reaction.

"You had it coming after your attack on Crammer. Despite what happened, he was a good agent." Sharn sat there amazed by Brett. She had expected him to apologise, or try to curry her favour. Instead, he'd stood his ground.

"Okay, we'll let that go, for now, let's eat." She suggested, getting up. Following her inside Brett watched her arse sway rhythmically as she moved to the table. He had to admit his first impression of her being his type had been correct, as looking closer he saw no outline of underwear in her dress. Concentrating on the table, he found two sets of plates and utensils laid out.

"What did you cook?"

"Nothing, I ordered some Chinese, I can't cook to save my life." She giggled.

"Yeah, it's not my forte either." Brett smiled, as Sharn took several containers from the oven, placing them on the table. In between eating their meal and stealing glances at her body, Brett brought her up to date on his progress. He admitted that he'd hit a dead end, till he'd sold his soul to the CIA.

"What do you think their angle is?" She asked.

"I'm not sure, but it's going to cost me somewhere soon in the future."

"What's your next move then?"

"Find the bad guys; kill the bad guys. Hopefully without getting killed myself. It's a straightforward plan, but usually effective. We've got a week and we know they're here somewhere, that's all I've got to work with." He admitted.

"I can help you there at least." She smiled. "The third unknown group you're looking for is a cartel from South America. Its run by a warlord named Corteze who headed up a syndicate made up of drug groups all over the world. He won't show up on our crims sheets because his not wanted in the States. A friend of mine over in Homeland security told me about him a couple of weeks ago. They were looking into a money-laundering scheme he was running. He wanted to know if we had anything. I kept a picture just in case, so I know it's him."

"Any idea where a thug like him would hang out?" Brett asked, impressed.

"No, but he's a high roller. He wouldn't stay somewhere unless it's the best. I'd try the top hotels or the high-end rental properties. You can bet he's got plenty of loot with him, he doesn't want for anything."

"That's a big help, thank you," Brett answered, meaning it.

"We're both on the same side Brett. If you want something just ask me, I will give it." She replied a small smile on her lips, as silence followed her offer.

Brett visualised reaching across the table and ripping that dress right off her. Down below he felt his brainless head awakening to her offer. 'It's a trap' his real brain yelled, as Sharn, sat awaiting his answer, her nipples standing to attention through her dress. 'She had planned this whole seduction' he mused, his big head wanting to leave, his small head wanting to stay. Luckily his big head won.

"Look you've been a great help, but I'd better get going. This new lead will really help," He said standing. At first, Sharn was too surprised to reply. Standing with him, she silently walked him to the door.

"Goodnight Brett. I really enjoyed tonight. There's a lot more to you than I was led to believe." She smiled, giving him a light kiss on his cheek, as he entered the lift.

"I enjoyed it too." He stammered out, as the lift closed on Sharn.

Sharn stood looking at the lift for some time, before walking back to her lounge chair on the balcony. Pouring a glass of wine she sat down, thinking about her night with Brett. He was far more intelligent than she'd thought she smiled, sipping her wine. Most men would've stayed and been well satisfied after she'd worked her magic. He'd seen through her, something that didn't happen often.

Looking out over the ocean she realised she had enjoyed his company, liking him. Given the right circumstances, she knew she could love a man like Brett. On the other hand, unfortunately, he was a threat to her career, and that came first. Still, she smiled, next time she'd convince him to stay, and with luck, it would be soon.

Brett drove aimlessly after leaving Sharn's apartment. Frustrated, needing a drink he thought about returning to Sharn's apartment and what waited for him there. For some reason, which baffled him, he ended up outside the bar Linda worked in.

"I'll just go in and have one drink." He lied to himself, reaching for the door handle." 'It won't be one' his mind warned him making him hesitate. Any other time, he knew that he wouldn't have worried about the consequences. Knowing Adrian depended on him held him in check. Sitting in the car park, he stared at the clubs entrance unable to get out. Sobbing quietly, he lay across his front seat, falling into a deep sleep.

Linda, her shift over left the club. After another night of slobbering drunks, she was looking forward to getting home. Her dream of getting out of this dump kept her going as she walked towards the corner to catch her bus. Glancing in the car park, she saw the black sedan sitting on its own in the corner of the block. It had Fed's written all over it, as she curiously strolled across to it.

Looking inside she saw Brett lying dejectedly across the seat. Tapping on the glass, she watched him slowly open his eyes, before swiftly sitting up looking embarrassed.

"Are you okay?" she asked concerned, as Brett opened his door.

"Linda, I didn't know where to go?" he murmured his crumpled appearance, making him look lost and defenceless.

"You haven't drunk anything have you?" she asked softly bending down next to the window.

"No, but it was a close thing. I came here to have one, but the thought of Adrian being out there somewhere hurt stopped me." Brett confessed.

"Have you heard anything?"

"We've got some leads, I'm hoping one pans out." He answered looking better.

"Well since you're here, how about a lift?" she smiled, without waiting for an answer, she walked to the passenger side getting in.

The drive to Linda's unit was filled with unsaid emotions as each person waited for the other to say something. Pulling up at Linda's place Brett cut the engine, as they both sat unmovingly. Brett in the end spoke.

"You're the best thing that's happened to me in a long time Linda. I wish I could be with you always, I just don't trust myself to make you happy." Linda sat there stunned by Brett's confession; it took her several seconds to reply.

"I know you've been through a lot Brett, but if you think you can get by on your own without help, you're kidding yourself. I tried it once, it doesn't work. Everyone needs love, Brett, let me try, I need you too." she cried her head falling into her lap, as she sobbed. Reaching across Brett lifted her up, pulling her to him.

"Let's go inside?" He whispered as he pulled her across to his side of the car, helping her out. Smiling Linda was just about to say thank you for helping her out, when he pulled her into his arms, kissing her. Although they'd kissed many times before, Linda sensed that this time with him it was different, as if he was giving all of himself, not holding back. Breaking their embrace, Linda saw a tear forming in the corner of Brett's eye, which he wiped away, appearing embarrassed by it.

"I love you, Brett."

"And I love you too Linda," Brett confessed, as holding hands like teenagers on their first date, they hurried inside.

PARTNERS

Corteze sat beside the pool, overlooking LA from the hills above. He had rented an ex-movie stars house, down on his luck, for a small fortune. From this tucked away location, his men had been looking for 'The Cuban'. Assassins were a hard group to locate and finding this Cuban was proving difficult. Through a lowlife drug peddler, they'd made contact with him, arranging to call him on a number supplied.

The guy was clever wanting no upfront meeting, just a swap meet. He'd given them a location where the swap would occur, once the money was paid of course. The money to Corteze was secondary, the scientist and his research were everything. What he didn't like, was being led around by his nose by this assassin. As head of the Cartel, he should've been given more respect from this lowlife. This Cuban treated him with contempt; he needed to learn his place in the scene of things. Looking across at Felix, he saw him chatting on the phone his eyes watching Corteze.

"He is getting sloppy," Corteze said to himself, remembering the botched attempt on Jamal and Son Tang. As head of security letting them escape was bad enough. To allow them to escape using Corteze's own plane was unforgivable. Now the woman they had on the inside was dead and the files gone. Felix was getting old Corteze realised, deciding that after this trip was over, he would be retired permanently.

For now, all that mattered was getting the scientist and his research. He'd wear being disrespected by the Cuban, as long as he got what he wanted.

Felix watched his boss feeling his usefulness slipping away. The chances of him getting home after his stuff up of the hit on Jamal and Son Tang was fifty-fifty. With the further loss of the files, it was now zero. Needing air, he walked out to the front gate, passed the two guards stationed there. Explaining he was just going for a walk, Felix walked down the road to a small park. Sitting on a bench, he weighed up his options lighting a much-needed cigar, relaxing.

"How are you, Felix?" A voice asked as a large man sat down beside him. Looking up, shading his eyes to see, Felix watched Jamal seat himself next to him. Momentarily surprised Felix, in the end, chuckled, knowing his death was no longer in Corteze's hands.

"It amazed me how easily you escaped our trap. How did you ever think to bring a rope?" Felix asked.

"Kabal my security man was responsible. He had every man carry something different just in case."

"He is a good man to have at your back Jamal. I warned Corteze of the danger of trying to wipe out so many Cartels at the same time. It was to no avail, as he is obsessed with obtaining the research for the Blight."

"What is he planning?" Jamal asked. Felix at first sat there stunned by Jamal's question. He was asking him candidly to betray his boss.

"Why would I tell you, Jamal? Chances are I won't even be leaving this park alive." He laughed.

"I give you my word, that if you tell me truthfully what Corteze is planning, you can go free," Jamal told him, stopping his laughter. Felix thought over Jamal's offer carefully. He was putting his life on the line, on the word of a drug smuggler. Thinking back Felix went over all he knew about Jamal. True he had a reputation for violence and when crossed showed no mercy. On the other hand, he'd never heard anyone question his word, something that was rare in their line of work.

"Okay Jamal, though it astounds me that I would do it, I will take you at your word." Felix smiled, telling him everything.

"So he doesn't know who this Cuban is?" Jamal asked having listened to Felix explain Corteze's whole plan.

"If he is really an assassin or just someone who was lucky enough to capture the scientst we're not sure. But he does have him that is all that matters."

"So you're just going to hand over a hundred million dollars to a phantom. Corteze must be crazy?"

"We had planned to cover the drop-off point where the Cuban arranged to meet with us. Even if they already have the money, it won't stay theirs for long."

"Thank you, Felix, you've upheld your end of the bargain. Go in peace, my friend." Jamal smiled, as Felix stood up, walking out of the park. Hesitating Felix looked back at Jamal before nodding a goodbye and walking down the hill towards LA.

"You're letting him go?" Kabal exclaimed having observed the meeting.

"Yes my friend, I gave my word."

"Felix is a clever man. Is it wise to let him go free?

"He is finished, my friend. Let him take what money he's hidden away and retire. I see no reason to kill a man for no reason." Kabal was just about to bring up another point why Felix should be killed when Jamal stopped him. "The reason why he lives is so he will pass along that my word is to be honoured. In the future, when I swear if someone, that if they cross me, I will get revenge, they will heed my warning. Trust is something to be valued, my friend."

"The men are ready Jamal," Kabal said, moving on.
"Okay, let's finish this business."

"Where is Felix?" Corteze asked Jose, one of his bodyguards.
"He told one of the men at the front door he was going for a walk."
"Get him back here now!" Corteze ordered. Walking into the house, Jose told the two men guarding the front door to go and get him. Obeying the two men opened the front door, to a storm of gunfire.

Jamal's men had just starting to move into position when the front door opened. Corteze's two men caught off guard went for their weapons, as Jamal's men surged forward, opening fire. Retreating back inside, Cortezes men, both fatally hit, slammed the door, collapsing onto the floor. Jamal's men undeterred, rushed to the door, slamming into it. The door, unfortunately, had been specially constructed for the movie star owner. Four inches thick, with a steel frame; it resisted Jamal's men's battering.

Undeterred Kabal swiftly planted an explosive charge against it. Backing away from the door, Kabal detonated the charge caving the door in. Opening fire as they entered, the whole house became a battlefield as opposing cartel gunmen fought for control. Jamal knew Corteze had ten men with him, while his group, numbered twenty. In a fight like this, tactic mattered very little in the end; it came down to who had the most guns.

Corteze also knew the power of numbers. Seeing the tide of battle move against him, he ordered Jose to lead his men forward. Corteze then used the diversion to sneak out the back door. Once clear of the house, he ran to the rear of the property, where he had left a vehicle, in case of an emergency. It shamed him to leave his men behind to die. On the other hand, he could always get more men he smiled, as he quickly jumped into the sedan.

A shot fired through the front windscreen slammed him back into the seat. Looking down at his expensive Armani shirt, he watched a large red stain spread over his chest. It was then that the pain hit him. Screaming in agony, he tried to raise his hand to open the door, only to find his limbs didn't respond.

"Help me!" he shouted, as a shape blocked the sun next to his window.

"You were always arrogant Corteze. Did you really think you kill all those men and there be no consequences? You are a fool." Jamal exclaimed, turning to walk away, as the sound of sirens could be heard in the distance.

"How did you know about this vehicle?"

"Felix told me. He's now on his way home after telling me everything." Jamal chuckled, leaving Corteze cursing the day Felix was born.

When the report of a shooting came in between two large groups of men, one of Brett's response teams rushed to the location. After identifying Corteze's group, they called Brett. He'd spent the night with Linda and was happily making them both breakfast when his phone rang. He was told that twelve bodies had been recovered from the house; two were identified as part of the group run by Muhammad Jamal. The big news was Corteze, the cartel leader, was still alive.

Upon finding the Cartel leader still alive, Brett issued a release to the media informing them that Corteze, along with a large group of men had been found dead. While this was occurring, he had Corteze rushed to a local hospital under an assumed name and a heavy police guard. Telling Linda what had occurred and seeing how excited he was, she told him to forget breakfast and get going. Kissing her promising to ring, he bolted for the door.

When Brett arrived at the hospital, he was told Corteze had only hours to live. Shot in the chest, his condition was critical, as he slowly bled to death. Brett thought long and hard about how to question this man, in the end, he decided to go with the truth. Approaching Corteze's room, he like everyone else, showed his ID before being allowed to enter. Brett took one look at the white near bloodless body of Corteze and knew hours was being optimistic.

"I'm not going to bullshit you Corteze, you're fucked. Anything you want to tell me before you continue on to your appointment with Satan?" Corteze at first seemed confused by Brett's statement, he recovered quickly.

"Rot in hell Fed. Why should I tell you anything, like you say, I'm not going to be around long?" He chuckled, before coughing up blood. Brett seeming unfazed by his answer, sat down on the bed beside him.

"Yeah but Jamal is. His most probably got the scientist by now." Corteze didn't reply, he just lay there staring at Brett, as if his concentration was elsewhere.

"Did you hear me Corteze or are you just stupid?"

"I heard you pig, and he can't have him yet, the meeting is not for another 2 hours." He coughed out before continuing. "Can you promise me you'll put a bullet in Jamal and Felix?"

"I can guarantee to try, will that do?" Brett told him smiling.

"Good enough. He's meeting the Cuban at a shopping mall called The Beverly centre. I'm not sure where in the centre they are meeting, Felix had those details." He coughed again before going still.

"He's gone, Sir." The nurse whispered beside him, as Brett stood up.

"Burn in hell you lowlife arsehole," Brett exclaimed, startling the people there, as he swiftly grabbed his phone. Calling the Situation room, he ordered them to send every man they had to the shopping centre pronto.

"Hang on Adrian." He whispered, running to his car.

THE SWAP

While Brett sent his men towards the shopping centre, Jamal was already there setting up. He had ten of his original twenty men with him. Five were dead the others either injured or looking after them. The meet was in the blue section car park on the second level. To Jamal, it seemed like a strange place for an exchange. Inside in the crowd would've been far better for this Cuban. Here he risked being killed once the trade was completed.

Jamal knew the money would be gone as soon as he handed them the bank account number and that's what worried him. There was no reception here, how did the Cuban expect to check the account when he couldn't communicate?

"He's an amateur." Jamal smiled. Positioning his men, he gave orders, that no one opened fire until the scientist was in their hands.

Two hours passed slowly, as Kabal and Jamal waited near the entrance to the mall, opposite the Blue section of the car park. Jamal, like Kabal beside him, felt exposed. An American shopping centre wasn't the place for two men of Arabic appearance to be seen loitering around. Many of the shoppers gave them a wide berth, as they entered and left the mall, Kabal became worried.

"You'd think we were both carrying grenades and rifles, by the way, they stare at us."

"Yes, the World Trade Tower fiasco has severely affected them." Jamal smiled, thinking of how threatening their food supply, would break them. Looking across at Kabal he saw him pick up his phone listening. His eyes showed alarm.

"Our men on the other side of the mall report that a group of heavily armed police have arrived." Jamal stood there thinking for several minutes before answering.

"How many men are on that side?"

"Only three Jamal."

"Have them opened fire on the police and draw them away from this side," Jamal ordered as a black van stopped opposite them. The van he noticed had heavily tinted windows and no rear window. This presented him with a problem, having no idea how many people were in the van. From where Jamal stood the van had nosed into the wall opposite making approaching the van from this side's sliding door and the rear door the only options.

"Is this them?" Kabal whispered, as in reply, a hand appeared at the slightly opened side door, waving them forward. Both of them moved towards the van, as in the distance, Jamal heard the sound of gunfire erupting in the mall. 'They can't hear it above their engine running' Jamal thought, as a hand signal told them to stop about twenty paces short of the van.

"That's close enough. Throw the bank account number to us." A voice with a slight accent commanded.

"Where's the scientist first?" Kabal shot back. The door suddenly flew right open revealing three figures. Two were dressed in black wearing ski masks and carrying submachine guns. The other was tied up, from a picture Jamal had seen; he knew it was the scientist. Jamal felt Kabal beside him prepare to draw his pistol and spring forward, as the door again closed, leaving a small gap.

"Be at peace Kabal. Give them the account number." He ordered. Kabal relaxing, slowly pulled out the USB stick, tossing it into the van.

"Give us ten minutes to check it, and you can have him." The Cuban told them slamming the door. In the distance, Jamal noticed the shooting had stopped, as a stream of people rushed from the Mall.

"Tell the men to be ready Kabal. They'll realise soon that they can't get a signal. Then they'll either bluff their way out pretending they did, or they'll make a run for it." Jamal pointed out, moving back behind a car opposite.

Five minutes passed, and the standoff continued. Kabal's phone ringing startled them both.

"What is it?" Jamal barked angrily.

"The police are sweeping the building, they will be here soon."

"We've no time left, rush the van," Jamal ordered. Four of their men, who had slowly crept up behind the adjoining vehicles, surged to their feet running to the van. Smashing the side window a smoke grenade was tossed in, as a dull bang sounded from the van. Smoke billowed out the broken window as Jamal's men ripped open the side door. Behind them shoppers fled screaming, fearing the terrorists, were in the car park on this side as well.

Jamal joining his men, stared into the van as the smoke cleared, finding no one there. Surprised he saw a door on the opposite side, up against the wall. Opening it he found the van had parked up against a fire door, which was opened.

"They have outsmarted us!" Jamal screamed, as a call to drop their weapons, bellowed out behind them.

"Run Jamal!" One of his men yelled as the man turned, throwing a smoke grenade behind them. Kabal beside Jamal seeing he was distracted, still staring at the fire door, grabbed him. Pushing him forward through the van, they tumbled into the fire escape as an avalanche of gunfire cascaded through the thick smoke which surrounded them. Behind them obscured in the cloud of smoke, Jamal's four men gave their lives for him, to give him a chance to escape.

"We must run Jamal. There is no time to think about what has happened." Kabal shouted in his ear, as bullets ricocheted off the walls above them.

"Lead the way my friend and forgive me for hesitating. What of my men?"

"They are dead Jamal. Let's not let their martyrdom be for nothing." Kabal told him as they both rushed down the stairwell. Exiting in the car park below, they ran towards the exit as Kabal tried the doors of cars parked there. Becoming desperate, knowing they were in the open, they decided to run back into the Mall. There at least they could blend in. Two men of Arab appearance with pistols running was sure to attract attention. People already fleeing the shootout inside started to scream when they saw them.

Turning a corner, their luck ran out as two police officers behind a police car called for them to halt. In the open, Jamal knew trying to escape was futile. Dropping his weapon, telling Kabal to drop his as well, they both raised their hands. One officer came forward handcuffing them, before picking up their discarded weapons.

Shoving them into the police car, they hit the siren, racing out of the car park.

Two police cars had the exit sealed. Instead of stopping their car, their captors rammed the other two police cars, accelerating away. Several shots rang out behind them, one smashing the rear window, as Jamal and Kabal sat there stunned at their captor's behaviour. The cops, in turn, started chuckling, at their reaction. Looking at the two cops, it suddenly occurred to Jamal that they were both of Asian appearance.

"Are you Son Tang's men?" Jamal asked as Kabal looked sideways at him.

"Yes, and you're lucky we got there in time." One answered in rough English, as they killed the siren. Slowing down blending into the traffic they travelled for about twenty minutes, before turning down a deserted side road. Driving slowly making sure there was no tail, they turned into an abandoned warehouse. Coming to a stop, the two imposter cops jumped out. Running back to the entrance, they closed the old roller door, before returning.

Opening their doors, they undid Jamal and Kabal's handcuffs telling them to follow them. When they failed to move, one of the men came back to them.

"Your men are all gone. The ones you left at your hideout have been warned by our men so they will have fled. You either come with us, or you're on your own. It's up to you."

"You have been following us?" Kabal exclaimed.

"Yes. You might be warriors back in your own country, but in LA, Son Tang's gangs control the city. We have followed you from the start. Even, when you raided Corteze's home, taking care of him, we were there. That is why you are alive; Son Tang owes you for his demise."

Kabal looked to Jamal awaiting his decision.

"It seems we owe Son Tang our lives lets go thank him," Jamal answered smiling.

When Brett arrived at the exchanges location, he found one of his Swat units already engaged. As ordered they had entered the shopping centre, looking for any of Jamal's cartel men. Without warning, they'd been fired upon. A heated firefight took place with three men being shot and captured. All were alive, while four shoppers and a Swat member had also been hit.

Brett came to the conclusion that it was a delaying tactic, so he ordered all units to sweep the building. It wasn't easy as thousands of shoppers hearing the shot raced for the exits. It was like being hit by a tidal wave, as his men tried to keep some form of order. Leaving local police officers to stop people being trampled to death in their haste to leave, the FBI continued to search.

Behind them, the crowd thinning allowed medics to attend the hurt. It was during this time that they got their first break. A woman had reported two men of Arabic appearance on the second level car park, on the opposite side of the Mall. Sending the majority of men in that direction, Brett as well followed suspecting this was the exchange location.

They arrived just in time to see six men attacking a van. Brett had wanted to open fire without warning, but a local Sergeant with a blow horn had called for their surrender. One turned and lobbed a smoke grenade between the van and his force, causing confusion, as the suspects opened fire. Luckily some of the swat team had thermal sights, allowing them to shoot accurately through the smoke, reducing casualties amongst his men.

Still, when the smoke cleared they had three men down, none seriously hurt. Four of the shooters were dead, the other two unaccounted for. A search soon revealed the hidden fire escape.

"Fuck we nearly had them all!" Brett yelled giving the Sergeant with the blow horn, an angry look. Continuing the search, ordering all exits blocked, he handed over the scene to the forensics team. Ten minutes later he received the report that a police car had rammed the roadblock, escaping. Immediately Brett asked for all helicopters in the area, police or private to try and find the rogue police vehicle.

They got their second break when a local TV station helicopter, spotted the police car entering a disused factory. Calling in additional units, they surrounded the warehouse finding the car inside empty. That dead-ended the operation.

PAYING THE PIPER

Brett sat at his desk going over the reports from the shootout and the following chase. He was looking for something, anything that would give him a lead to Adrian. He knew from DNA in the van that Adrian had been there. It was clear the swap had gone down, but not what had occurred. Did one of the drug cartels have him now, or was it a bust and the Cuban still held him? Time was running out, and the exchange already arranged with the Cuban was in two days' time.

The only good news was Jamal's gang had been rounded up, trying to leave LA. It appeared Jamal after wiping out Corteze's men, had taken over the swap. Raul, his accountant had been left to look after the injured, from the raid in Jamal's absence. Someone had tipped him off that the swap had gone badly, and he had organised to fly the injured men out on an aircraft he had purchased. He nearly succeeded.

Taking off from a small airfield in an old twin-engine beachcomber he flew out over the ocean towards Hawaii. Unfortunately for him, someone at the airport saw him loading the injured and connected the dots to the Mall shootout. A Navy fighter after firing some warning shots convinced him to return. Landing at an Airforce base Raul and his men started their lifetime terms in maximum security.

Raul was not a fool though. He refused to say anything, knowing Jamal's reputation first hand for dealing with traitors. The big question was what had happened to Jamal and his right-hand man Kabal? Brett realised sadly that he was back to square one. His mobile phone ringing made him jump. Looking at the ID of the person ringing he saw a blank. 'Who knows my number?' he thought as he answered it.

"Good morning Mr Heckle, or can I call you Brett?" Brett didn't have to ask who it was, he knew the devil's voice.

"I suppose this is when I pay my debt?" He answered waiting.

"Jamal and Kabal are being held by Son Tang and his gang, on an old freighter in the harbour, named the Golden maiden. When you raid the ship, we want Jamal dead, and Kabal set free. Do you understand?"

"Yeah, I get it. What's Kabal to you?"

"None of your business, is it a deal?"

"I gave my word. You can," was all he got out as the line went dead.

"You piece of shit!" Brett screamed, silencing the room.

"Everything okay Brett?" Dan asked watching him.

"I'm okay Dan. Just got a tip telling me where Jamal is, from one of the demons." He smiled.

"You need some lubricant?" Dan laughed.

"Very funny Dan." Bret chuckled. "Now gather the men. We've got some bad guys to bring in." Brett told him, calming down, wondering how hot hell was.

Son Tang like Jamal thought honour amongst thieves was rare but necessary to a leader. That was why he had spared Jamal and Kabal and warned his men. Now he sat with the two men discussing their next move.

"As much as it pains me to admit it, this Cuban fellow outsmarted me at the exchange," Jamal confessed suppressing his anger.

"Yes, he seems to have planned the whole operation with the one objective of getting the money and holding onto the scientist." Son Tang put forward.

"But why would he do such a thing?" Kabal asked.

"There is a rumour around the town that the US Government is negotiating for the scientist's release. Maybe he intends to gain more money from them as well?" Son Tang suggested.

"His greed will be his downfall. The Americans have far better ways of tracking the transfer of money than we have. Still, I would like to see him succeed against the Americans; it would make me being fooled more palatable." Jamal smiled.

"Unfortunately, we are all known to the authorities. Our chance of obtaining this scientist, is now dead. We must leave LA immediately before we too are detained or killed." Son Tang pointed out before continuing. "This ship is due to leave in two days. Although it is not the Ritz, I would suggest that you two travel with us back to Asia. From there you can arrange transport back to Pakistan." Seeing both men nod their consent, Son Tang had one of his men, show them to their rooms.

Once the men had left, Son Tang gathered his men, giving instructions to treat Jamal and Kabal with the same respect that they gave him. Going over their areas of patrolling before they left port, he walked onto the deck having a quick look around. In the distance, he saw two black helicopters travelling back and forwards across the harbour, stopping every now and then before continuing.

'Some sort of training exercise,' he told himself as the helicopters did another movement coming closer.

Looking down onto the deck, he saw several of his men were watching the two choppers as well. Most carried pistols hidden under their clothing, though some had assault rifles. Son Tang smiled, seeing all their weapons were well hidden as he had instructed. With another loop, the choppers again crossed the harbour, growing closer.

A feeling of something being not quite right, gripped him, as he realised the two helicopters, would next time pass right overhead. Shouting a warning to his men proved fruitless, as the two choppers drown out his shouts, as, without warning, they dropped onto the deck. Black dressed men exploded from the choppers, as stun grenades flashed amongst Son Tang's surprised men. Most were now down on the deck being secured, as the invading armed men spread out over the ship.

Running for a hatchway, Son Tang dived through it as bullets impacted on the steel door frame. Pulling out his pistol he fired several shots back through the door, before closing the steel door and locking it. Running along the passageway he encountered two of his men standing in the passageway looking confused.

"Hold the passageway as long as you can. Surrender only when you think you have no alternative." He told them, wishing them good luck, knowing his men dying wouldn't change anything. Leaving them, he raced to Jamal's cabin, deciding it was time for them to all leave.

Jamal too was aware there was a problem. The Swat team that had landed on the ship might have been using silenced weapons, but Son Tang's men were not. Kabal hearing the gunfire had advised Jamal to move to the rear of the ship, as the main exchange of fire still seemed to be at the centre and towards the bow. Nodding his consent, Jamal was just following Kabal out, when Son tang arrived.

"Come with me, I have a small rubber boat moored at the side towards the bow," he informed him, moving ahead not waiting for an answer.

"Is that wise wouldn't it be better to head to the rear of the ship?" Kabal put in, stopping Son Tang.

"And what would you do once you reached there? The gangplank to the shore is located at that end of the ship, surely this raids Commander would have men boarding there at this very moment." Son Tang pointed out, looking at Kabal. Jamal saw Kabal seemed about to say something instead he followed Son Tang.

Son Tang had been surprised by Kabal's lack of foresight. He had heard and seen him react swiftly to situation at the airport when they'd seised Corteze's plane. Why now was he suggesting a course of action, which would've got them all killed or captured? Another thought came to Son Tang. How did the American's discover his hiding place? He'd been here for over three weeks, yet it was only one day since Kabal and Jamal had boarded, and now they'd been discovered. 'Could Kabal be setting Jamal up,' he asked himself.

Arriving at a sealed door in the ships side Son Tang with Kabal's help opened it. Below them floating peacefully, was a rubber dingy. The weapons fire that had chased them through the ship had petered out. Single shots could still be heard, but organised resistance was over.

"Kabal can you check the corridors behind us, while I prepare the boat?" Son Tang asked as with a nod Kabal disappeared back down the passage. As soon as he had moved off, Son Tang and Jamal climbed down into the dingy.

"Do you trust Kabal?" Son Tang asked once they were seated.

"Of course, why do you ask?" Jamal answered, surprised by the question.

"How did the police find us? And going towards the rear, why did he suggest that?" Son Tang whispered as Jamal sat thinking. Kabal had been his top man for over 5 years. No one did he trust more, yet he had to admit lately he'd been distant as if waiting for something to happen. Still, they'd been through a lot together Jamal owed him his life; he'd need more than suspicions to judge his friend.

"We'll discuss it later," Jamal said as Kabal appeared above them.

"The coast is clear let's go." He said softly climbing in beside Jamal, as Son Tang started the motor. Moving along the side of the ship keeping the engine noise to a minimum, Son Tang edged the dingy under the adjoining wharf near the bow heading away from the ship. The helicopters had been his biggest worry, now hidden by the wharf he increased speed.

"Do you have a phone Kabal? I left mine aboard the ship." Son Tang whispered watching Kabal.

"No, I too forgot to bring mine. Kabal answered. Jamal beside him remained quiet. Son Tang was fishing Jamal realised. At first, he'd been angry, with Son Tang's tactics in accusing Kabal. Now as he sat there he remembered Kabal grabbing his phone and gun from the bedside table before they left the room.

Reaching for his own weapon he looked ahead to see a set of timber steps coming down to the waters edge through the wharf itself. Cutting the engine Son Tang steered the dingy next to the stairs as the three men silently stepped onto the first timber plank. Jamal instantly pushed his gun into Kabal's back.

"Hand over your weapon my friend," Jamal ordered.

"Jamal, what is wrong?" Kabal whispered as Son Tang stepped up beside him.

"Empty your pockets." Son Tang snarled. Kabal at first made to comply, when he suddenly he headbutted Son Tang, knocking him to the ground. He was reaching for his gun, when Jamal behind him, hit him across the back of his neck, making him collapse back into the dingy. Helping Son Tang up, Jamal, both ashamed and disgusted with his supposed friend, searched through his pockets finding his phone.

"I cannot believe you betrayed me?" Jamal sobbed, Son Tang saw he was crestfallen at his friend's betrayal.

"What did you tell them, traitor? You have ten seconds to tell me before I cut your throat." Son Tang threatened, drawing his knife.

"Everything, unfortunately." A voice shouted, above them, as two gunshots echoed around the wharf area.

When Brett was told of Son Tang's location, he with the help of his team planned the raid. While the choppers slowly wove a pattern backwards and forwards across the bay, Brett moved his men along the wharf. Stationing them just beside the boarding ramp, they waited till the signal from the chopper telling them they had landed. Once the go signal had been received, Brett's men on the wharf surged onto the vessel.

Overpowering the men stationed there they swept the ship eliminating all the opposition. It was when they were nearing the end of their search that Brett's phone had rung. It was his friend Mr Brown of the CIA. He told him Jamal and Son Tang were escaping by boat from the bow of the ship. Rushing back of the ship, leaving his men to continue the sweep, Brett ran to the bow. As he arrived, he saw the tail of the rubber dingy disappear under the wharf.

Running flat out along the wharf, he arrived at the steps as Jamal and Son Tang disarmed Kabal. Common sense told him to take them alive, his deal with the devil made him fire. Kabal stood there frozen, as Son Tang and Jamal tumbled into the water, both lying face down. Brett's gun remained locked on Kabal waiting.

"Thank you" He said in broken English, surprrised to be alive.

"I judge you work for us?"

"Yes although I shouldn't have told you." Kabal smiled.

"Better hit the road, those shot would've been heard," Brett told him, lowering his gun. Without another word, the man named Kabal ran into the night.

Although a lot of drugs were discovered on the vessel, Adrian's whereabouts were still unknown. Cursing, having to shoot two good leads, Brett, after giving his men a well done, returned to the Situation Room. Time he knew was running out, and after seeing this Cuban character doublecross the drug cartels, he wondered how they could trust him.

THE EXCHANGE

Brett stood solemnly watching the square. They were in downtown LA, across from a major crossroad in the city centre, waiting for the drop-off. Every roof surrounding the square held snipers, all waiting their chance to spot the kidnappers and take them out. The exchange was just ten minutes away, and still no sign of Adrian.

"Does anyone see anything?" he asked into his headset. No answer came, as his phone rang. "Who is it?"

"We want the bank account number now!" A voice demanded.

"Where's Adrian?"

"He is right in front of you Agent Heckle. Give me the number, or we take him elsewhere." The voice threatened.

"If you're lying, I'll find you no matter where you go," Brett promised, before reeling off the account numbers. As soon as he finished the sequence, the phone went dead.

Looking around again seeing nothing, Brett asked again if anyone had anything, no matter how small. After a few seconds of silence, one agent reported a bum having a fit in the alley across from them. Brett was just about to explode when picking up his binoculars, he focused on the hobo. He'd been laying there since they'd arrived. Someone had even suggested moving him, in case there was trouble. Brett had turned the request down, wanting nothing out of the ordinary to occur.

He did appear to be having a seizure, shaking badly; he'd even knocked off one of his shoes, Reeboks by the look.

"Reeboks!" Brett screamed, ordering everyone to secure the area, as he rushed across the road.

No bum could afford that type of footwear Brett cursed, as he reached the hobo. It was Adrian he realised, as he knelt down beside him, checking him for wires or bobby traps. Clear, he then checked his pulse, finding it erratic. Calling an ambulance, he stayed with Adrian while his team searched the area, trying to locate the kidnappers. They came up empty, they were long gone.

Brett accompanied Adrian to the hospital stationing guards at every entrance. He watched over him 24hrs a day, having Linda bring him a change of clothes. Adrian had been doped up on a mixture of drugs, including heroin. The doctors weren't sure what effect it would have on his mental or physical functions, only time would tell.

After two days, while hell was breaking lose at the agency for losing the money, Adrian woke up. At first, Brett saw understanding in his eyes, then fear seemed to grip him, as he crunched up in the foetal position. After watching several doctors examine him, Brett knew his friend would never be the same.

"Might be better to move him to a mental facility?" The chief doctor suggested, knowing they could do no more.

"Thanks, Doctor." Was all Brett could say.

Moving him for now, back to the University, Brett downhearted, returned to the FBI office. The Situation room was now empty, the operation had been closed down, and his team reassigned. Using a desk in the main office area, Brett went over the evidence gathered.

Everyone he noticed avoided him, as he went over every lead trying to find something to go on.

The only good thing was the Treasury Department was using their vast financial clout to trace the money. So far they had tracked it through a dozen dummy accounts slowly getting closer. Brett wished them luck although 100 million in the world of finance wasn't much to work with these days. Towards the afternoon, Brett received a message to meet Sharn in the Situation Room. When he arrived there, he found her waiting for him alone.

"How is Adrian?"

"Not good, his brains been fried. Doctors aren't sure if he'll pull through." Brett confessed. Sharn surmised that Brett was close to breaking.

"I'm sorry Brett, I really am, but I have to let you go. The President wants those responsible for losing the money punished. I can't help you." Brett could see she meant it.

"For what it's worth, I think you deserve your position here, you're intelligent and a good leader. You're also a beautiful woman." Brett told her, kissing her lightly on the lips, before leaving. Behind him, Sharn quietly wiped tears from her eyes.

Going back to the University, Brett devoted his time to looking after Adrian. Most staff there knew he'd been canned, but they let it slide. For over a week he tried to get something out of Adrian, to return him to his past life. It was all for nothing, as Adrian seemed capable of only handling the most basic of task. Linda on several occasions visited them as well. She missed Brett and wanted to help. She even looked after Adrian when Brett needed a break from watching him. The return of Dean Campbell brought Brett's stay to an abrupt end.

The President, desperate to reignite the research, released the Dean, hoping he could get Adrian focused again. When the Dean arrived and found Brett there, sparks flew. Brett was forcibly removed, as Dean Campbell put Adrian through the ringer, trying to break him loose. A week of everything from hypnosis to electric shock treatment, found Adrian unchanged. Admitting defeat the Dean had Adrian packed, dressed and sent to the Airport to return to Australia.

"Good riddance." The Dean shouted at Adrian, glad the guy responsible for all his problems was gone.

With Adrian's departure, Dean Campbell turned to their labs trying to rebuild Adrian's experiments from scratch. Andy at the nursery was told to go over the samples, to try and locate the DNA sequence Adrian had used. It was like finding a needle in a haystack. Andy tried everything coming up blank. Going over his research, he remembered one oddity, the sprinklers.

Going over the records again he found the sprinkler had activated earlier the night of the experiment. Checking the residue collected in the filters, he found that on the night of the experiment, a high rate of Sprayseed had been flushed through the pipes onto the weed blocks.

Sprayseed was a defoliating herbicide, used for killing weeds. It had been banned in many states, for its effect on humans. Checking it again to make sure, Andy couldn't believe he had missed it the first time. This meant that Adrian's blight hadn't worked, that someone had deliberately tampered with the experiment.

The question was what did he do? If the Dean found out he'd missed this tampering, he'd be fired for sure. On the other hand, the Dean was out of a job if he didn't find something. In the end, smiling, he decided to do nothing.

Senator Jefferies went about the week keeping away from the angry President. After the loss of the hundred million, it hadn't been wise to be near him. This fiasco had made him move up his retirement, knowing that now Adrian's blight was gone, the University would be short of money. The cost of running the security and logistics of the place was extraordinarily high. Now with the extra men and work hours caused by this mess, the bill would be phenomenal.

Questions might be asked as to where the funds were, questions the Senator wasn't prepared to answer. It was time to travel to his Geneva Bank and transfer the funds to somewhere untouchable. Phoning his office, he had the company jet prepared, telling his associates he was having some time off to recuperate.

While the Senator was travelling to Geneva, the Treasury Department finally located the hundred million. Checking the owner's identity came back with an answer no one believed. Checking it again, verifying it, they dutifully sent it to the President, and then waited for the explosion.

The President sat in the Oval office staring out the window, the message from the treasury held in his right hand.

"Are you a hundred percent sure about this?" He asked Jim, the head of the Secret service at the Whitehouse, his emotion just held in check.

"Yes, Sir. They checked it twice."

"It's just he's always been my advisor, I never thought he'd take advantage of his position like this."

"Everyone has their price Sir."

"I hope for all our sakes you're wrong Jim."

"Do you want him detained?"

"Where is he?"

"He's supposed to be having a break, but our sources tell us he's travelling to Geneva."

"What a coincidence. Get the proof and then arrest him. I want irrefutable evidence that it was his account." the President ordered.

"Yes, Sir."

"Jeffries a traitor; I've got to tell you it's hard to believe Jim."

"We'll soon know Sir," Jim replied, knowing from experience that this type of evidence was rarely proven wrong.

"One thing before you go, Jim. If he's guilty beyond doubt better, we keep this quiet, if you get what I mean?"

"Don't worry Sir. If he's guilty, I can promise you, he'll be dealt with swiftly."

"Thanks, Jim.' The President sa d softly knowing in an election year he couldn't allow a scandal to develop.

Brett getting a tip-off, of Adrian's move, rushed to the airport. Intercepting him as he was boarding Brett searched for something to say. He looked worn out and lifeless as Brett sputtered out an apology. He was sorry he failed his friend in not rescuing him from the Cuban. Linda to Brett's surprise, turned up as well, giving her support. In the end, Adrian's escorts insisted he board, ending their moment together.

"Goodbye, Adrian." Was all Brett could get out before he broke down completely. Linda supported him, as Adrian his expression blank was led away. Moving at the ramp, Adrian was just about to enter the boarding gate, when he turned and yelled, startling his escorts.

"Don't forget your ten percent!" He yelled back to Brett, making many of the passengers pull back frightened by his outburst. Adrian's guard caught by surprise moved in. Swiftly restraining him, they forced him forward, onto the plane, leaving Brett standing there broken.

Linda seeing the state Brett was in led him out to the car park. She was fearful for him, wanting to take him home. Assuring her he was okay and pointing out she had her own car to drive home, he allowed her to walk him to his vehicle.

"Don't give up on Adrian, he'll be okay, I'm sure of it." Linda burst out, startling him with her upbeat assessment of his friend's condition.

"I hope so Linda, but I've got to admit it doesn't look good." He confessed, secretly he given up hope of him recovering.

"He will surprise you I'm sure of it." Linda smiled before continuing. "What are your plans now?"

"Get a job somewhere. Although law enforcement is most probably a no-no?" He smiled.

"You'd make a great Private detective. Why don't you give that a try? I could help you set it up."

"Sounds good we'll talk about it later," Brett promised her, as hopping into his car, he started up. Smiling, Brett waved goodbye to her.

Driving back to his RV he stopped at the liquor shop, buying several bottles of bourbon. Fortified, he settled down for the night, slowly drowning his sorrows over Adrian's predicament.

GENEVA

Senator Jeffries alighted from his limo walking briskly into his bank. He was greeted by the bank manager himself, as was expected for a customer with such a large account. For some reason, he had the feeling he was being followed. Since landing in Geneva, he'd noticed several men in off the rack suits following him. In this town, he knew money was everything and for some reason, even though they were well dressed, their suits spoke of law enforcement, not business.

Still, as he was an important man to his country, maybe they'd been assigned by the President to protect him, he mused. The bank manager clearing his throat brought him back to the present. Nodding his attentiveness, he followed the manager to a secure room. The computer terminal here was as secure as you could get, being an inside system, independent of the banks outside computer network.

Gazing around the unfamiliar room, the Senator made sure there were no cameras, before entering his codes. He decided to wash his money through several accounts through the Isle of Man before returning the money to a shadow account in this bank. It seemed stupid to leave the money here, but he'd chosen this bank originally for its high security, seeing no reason to change.

Anyway once he'd washed the money through these accounts, the chances of anyone tracking it, was remote, to say the least. Keying in his instructions, he was just about to begin the transfers when he glanced at the high number of transfers his account had generated in the last few days. The twenty million, he'd moved from the University account, of course, was there. There were also two other transfers, both of a hundred million. Checking further he saw he also had a withdrawal, of one billion dollars!

Shocked, he frantically double checked his account, finding the amounts tallied. Both angry and scared he decided to check on where the two hundred million had come from. One amount he found was from South America, the other from LA. He then tried to trace where his billion had gone, finding it had been washed through accounts like he was just about to do, dead-ending it.

Somewhere in the back of his mind, the date in LA rang a bell, warning him of trouble. Using the bank's outside network, he checked the University's network regarding the investigation into Adrian's kidnapping. He found the time that the FBI handed over the money for Adrian, matched one of his transfers.

"I'm being set up!" Jeffries' concluded, as the realisation that the tail on him mightn't be for his protection, after all, dawned on him. What to do was his main concern' He knew the President wouldn't believe his side of it when the amount of money in his account came to light. With the money deposited in his account, he still had over seven hundred million plus change, which was serious money to disappear with. 'But how did they do it?' He asked himself perplexed by his account being hacked.

True he'd accessed the account regularly from the secure line in his office in Washington without any hitches so how'd they do it.

"The other day it didn't close down!" He shouted, before looking around, hoping he hadn't been heard. The last thing he needed now was anyone coming in here now to help he realised, settling down. 'Okay, I was hacked. How'd they find the access?' He mused. The only other place he kept access, was the University's secure network and that was as tight as a fish's arse.

He had personally had the system installed knowing it was better than the Whitehouse's to protect his own records. He then remembered how the President had told him of the young scientist's data being corrupted. Did someone not only corrupt the files but plant a worm? It made sense, meaning this wasn't a random thief, someone had deliberately targeted him. Why? Why go to all this trouble. This was personal he realised knowing his money wasn't all they wanted.

"Someone wants to destroy me. Well, they underestimated me." He smiled, coming up with a plan. Entering his account number, he transferred his entire account to the Isle of Man. Unlike before when he planned to transfer it back to this bank, he decided to leave it there, till he could move it somewhere else. Next, he had to disappear, anywhere of the grid. Many countries for various reasons, didn't allow extradition to America. The problem was, to find one with an acceptable level of luxury and freedom.

The Cayman Islands came to mind. It had a lavish lifestyle, for the rich and famous, while at the same time protecting them from countries that wanted their money or their imprisonment. Closing down his account and logging out, the Senator removed his phone from his pocket. Dropping it on the floor, he crushed it with his foot. Making sure he wasn't being watched, he left the computer terminal going to the men's restroom.

Several clients were in the cubicles, but their suit coats were hanging on hooks near the wash basins. His suit coat was dark in colour, so he exchanged it for a light grey suite hanging there. It was a little big on him, but wouldn't draw undue attention. Moving back to the entry door he peered out making sure no one was searching for him. Seeing nothing out of the ordinary, he moved towards the rear entrance, leaving. Bank security was tight, so he expected his shadows would be watching the front, where his limousine was waiting for him, rather than risk being spotted inside.

Hailing a cab, he decided against returning to his hotel, which would be obviously under surveillance. Opting instead to drive further into Europe, he decided to hire a car. As the driver drove him to a local hire car business, the Senator checked his suit pant's pocket. Relieved, he found that he was still carrying his spare passport. He always knew someday his plans might unravel, so he'd decided a long time ago to invest in some protection.

As part of a Senate investigation committee into a forging passport, Jeffries had found a friend. James Dudley had been a gifted forger, till the FBI had turned him. Travelling with Jeffries, he had shown him everything he knew about the fake passport industry. For his help, the FBI had cleaned his slate on the proviso he didn't forge American Passports.

Jeffries, after the committee had completed their work, returned to Dudley's place of business. He explained how sometimes it was necessary for him to travel of the radar. If Dudley believed him or not didn't matter, for a price he'd work for anyone. For a large, but fair amount of money, he'd made the Senator a perfect set of British identity papers and a passport.

Since the passport had a shelf life of ten years, it only had required the Senator to return once every eight years to Dudley to have it updated. It was the best insurance he'd ever bought. Examining the photo he saw despite it being five years old, he still looked the same. He knew that before boarding a flight he'd have to colour his hair slightly to throw off pursuers, but he couldn't see a problem. It was a small price to pay he chuckled, arriving at the car hire location.

He was just alighting from the cab when a black van screamed to a halt behind him. Panic seised him knowing who it was.

"The bastards must've been watching the rear entrance." He cursed looking for a way out. Jumping from the cab, he saw across the road a busy tourist market. 'If I can make that market I can still disappear' he smiled sprinting across the road.

The problem with Americans in Europe they never take the driving habits of the locals into consideration. The people in Geneva being mostly diplomatic or wealthy drove as if the roads belonged to them. As the Senator rushed out into the busy traffic, he underestimated the speed they were travelling at. Clipped by a passing Mercedes, he was spun around, losing his balance. Steadying himself, he took another step, right in the path of a Porsche.

The driver as at the time was rubbing his hand up the leg of his attractive companion, the last thing he expected was some fool to jump in front of him. The impact made a pulping noise as both the car and the Senator collided. The Senator came off second best, as he was thrown into the path of a bus travelling in the opposite direction. The multiple screams from the shoppers, told the Secret Service agents everything, as seeing the growing crowd, they retreated to their vehicle reporting the situation to their boss.

The Senator they informed him, had been taken care of permanently.

"I can't believe it. Seven hundred million dollars! That greedy, traitorous bastard." The President screamed, after reading a report on the Senator's bank account. "And the money is tied to the Cartel in South America and the Cuban kidnapper?" He continued, Jim just nodding yes. "Well at least we made a profit, that's something." He smiled wondering how he could use this extra money to bolster his coming election campaign.

"Sir, there's also the destruction of several Drug cartels and the arrest of over eighty of the world's top assassin's." The chief of the CIA piped in, trying to share the glory.

"You're right this is quite a coup. Thank everybody involved." The President beamed.

"The downside is the scientist's data has been lost. The Dean seems incapable of reproducing the DNA sequence." The head of the FBI added.

"He's a problem that man. Have him replaced, but do it quietly.

"What about the scientist and the FBI agent who headed up the investigation? Under the circumstances some compensation should be given to them." the Homeland Security boss chimed in.

"No the agent failed, he's out. The scientist from what I read is badly affected by his treatment. I don't want it connected in any way to this office. No communications with either of them whatsoever. Am I clear?" The President stormed as the meeting broke up.

Andy stood with Dean Campbell fencing off responsibility for the stuff up. The Dean was suspicious, he suspected Andy knew something.

"You've got ten seconds to tell me what you know, or you're fired. I can read you, man, you're guilty of something?" Andy knew as long as he kept his mouth shut he was safe. The problem was he was a lousy liar.

"I know nothing." He answered, watching the Dean smile.

"I've got you now Andy. Come clean, what do you know?" Andy feeling trapped hesitated, giving himself away. The Dean was just about to crack him when two of his security men arrived.

"Mr Campbell, you're wanted back at the office." One guard informed him.

"It's Dean Campbell to you!"

"Not anymore." The second guard told him, smiling.

"It seems you've been sacked. The new board of directors wants you off the premises immediately." The first guard snarled, as they moved in beside him, giving him no option than to go with them.

"There's been some mistake." Campbell pleaded, rattled by the development.

"Of course Sir, follow us please." The second guards politely instructed him, though it sounded more like an order.

"Have a good day Dean!" Andy yelled out, chuckling.

HONDURAS

TWO MONTHS LATER

Felix walked around the grounds of the luxury hotel complex stretching his legs. Since his return from America, he'd been busy. With the Cartel leadership decimated by Corteze, Felix had positioned himself to fill the void, taking over the control of several Cartels including Corteze's.

"It had been so easy." He chuckled to himself, going from being gotten rid of, to running the whole operation. Now word had spread, that the Asian Cartel formally run by Son Tang, was up for grabs. Jamal's second in command Kabal had taken over Jamal's organisation, but he seemed reluctant to move into Asia.

"He's a fool," Felix said out loud, having already sent some of his men to secure an agreement with Son Tang's family. It was all coming together, the only shadow hanging over them, was the blight. Rumours were the scientist who invented the gene virus was dead, his research lost. If that was true, the sky was the limit for Felix's global cartel.

Lighting up a well-deserved cigar, Felix contemplated his incredible luck in surviving Corteze's stupidity. His happy mood was interrupted by one of his ten security guards.

"Sir, Kabal is on the phone. He wishes to talk to you about Son Tang's cartel.

"He is too late, the fool." Felix laughed, thinking at last Kabal had realised his mistake.

Signalling for his man to pass him the phone, Felix prepared himself for the coming squabble. Holding all the cards, Felix decided to be fair with Kabal maybe giving him a 20 percent share in Son Tang's cartel, in return for the total control of distribution in the USA.

"Good morning Kabal how are you?" Felix started feeling confident.

"It is night here Felix but good morning to you as well," Kabal replied.

"I judge you want a share of Son Tang's cartel?"

"No, I want complete control of your entire operation." Kabal confidently answered, stopping Felix in his tracks.

"You don't have the money or the firepower my friend, so let's be civil about this, you don't want a war with me," Felix growled, all thought of cutting Kabal in gone.

"If you agree to go right now, with saying one hundred million dollars, I'll let you live," Kabal answered, sounding like he was making a significant concession.

"You're a dead man Kabal. Hiding in the Afghan mountains, won't save you this time." Felix spat out, furious.

"I'm sorry to hear that Felix. Goodbye, my friend say hello to Jamal and Son Tang for me." Kabal laughed, hanging up.

Felix beside himself with anger tossed the phone to the ground. 'I'll torture his whole family for this insult.' Felix told himself, picking the phone back up. Signalling to his security who were never far away, Felix decided to put a contract out on Kabal for the same amount they did for the scientist. Although that attempt had failed, it showed how affective it had been in getting assassins moving.

Dialing his contact in the local armed forces, he decided to increase his security here until Kabal was dead. As he made to dial, he saw a red dot flicker across his phones surface, before stopping on his chest. Too surprised even to scream out, Felix collapsed onto the ground shot through the heart.

Five hundred metres away Johnson lowered his weapon, crawling slowly over the ridgeline. He'd have to stay hidden here for at least a month he mused, knowing the cartel wouldn't take Felix's death well. Then again this operation had made him nearly half a million dollars and unlike the last one, this one he'd get paid for.

PRESENT DAY NEW ZEALAND

"What the fucks going on?" Brett repeated, as the group getting over his commando styled entrance, started to laugh.

"Can you let go of me, Brett? It's starting to hurt." Linda whispered as Brett getting over his surprise released her.

"Best sit down Brett and my names, not Andy, its Robbo." The Cuban smiled, throwing him his gun. "It's not loaded or a real gun. I knew with your training, you wouldn't walk on board without some persuasion."

Sitting down, more in shock than anything, Brett waited. In front of him now looking guilty, stood Linda, Emma, a Japanese looking young woman and a healthy looking Adrian.

"I'm sorry you were kept in the dark, but it was necessary." Adrian began. "I never told you about my father Brett, all this was about getting justice for him. My father was killed for his patents, back when I was just a boy. He worked for a Think tank University run by a Dean Jeffries. That same man is now a Senator and a partner of the American government, in the University. The same one you were assigned to and I study at.

I knew going to the law wouldn't help. So I devised a plan to bring Jefferies down, taking what he loved most, his wealth. With the help of my friends here in Australia and Linda, plus Emma towards the end, I succeeded in bringing him to justice."

"What did Linda and Emma have to do with this?" Brett interrupted, sounding angry.

"Linda helped in keeping me informed and ran interference for me. Like when you tried to intercept my kidnappers at the club, she distracted you at the bar allowing us entry. Emma got onto me, knowing I wasn't who I pretended to be."

"Yeah, and how did she do that?" The young Japanese woman asked, sounding upset.

"Kim you knew I had to pretend to be alone with no girlfriend. Even though, that was the most enjoyable part of my deception. Unfortunately, Emma figured out I was too confident, something I shouldn't have been." Adrian admitted getting a playful punch from Kim in return, showing she wasn't completely convinced.

"It was the best paid night I ever had." Emma giggled, giving Adrian a wink, avoiding Kim's scrutiny.

"Anyway, let's get back to your plan." Brett interrupted, still showing anger.

"While putting my research on the University network, I uploaded a worm with my program to study plant DNA. With it I traced the whereabouts' of Senator Jeffries' accounts, finding where he hid his wealth. Once I'd uncovered that I let the Dean know I was ready to test my blight. He in turn I knew, to advance his career and fortune, would tell the Senator.

Of course, once the Senator knew, I calculated he would get the President involved. His search for a way of hurting the drug cartels to help his re-election was critical to my plan. From what happened to you Brett, I figured the mole in the FBI would get wind of it and tell his Drug Cartel masters about such a serious threat.

Regrettably, the reward for my death was a lot higher than I thought possible. The generous offer for killing me brought out every assassin with a gun. The attempted hit on me made me advance my plan, arranging to be kidnapped in town instead of risking staying at the University. You telling me to leave enforced it for me.

Kim and Robbo then abducted me, with Linda's help. The rest was just a matter of setting up the druggies and then arranging my body to be dropped at the exchange."

"You could've died from an assassin's bullet or that overdose of heroin you idiot." Brett pointed out. He'd been worried by Adrian's state at the time.

"Yes, since none of you had experience with drugs it was a calculated risk you shouldn't have taken." Kim piped in, sounding upset.

"I'm sorry Kim, but it was necessary. Anyway, Linda kept an eye on me, knowing exactly what I'd taken." Adrian explained, although Kim still looked upset.

"You were lucky my friend. There could've been serious side effects." Robbo pointed out.

"Moving on." Adrian wanted to get away from the subject. "Once the Cartel paid their money, and the Government paid theirs, we transferred the funds into the Senators account knowing the Treasury Department would trace it eventually. And that, in a nutshell, is what I did." Adrian admitted, waiting for Brett to respond. The room now went silent as all eyes turned to Brett.

"I can see your motive Adrian, but you put a lot of lives at risk. What about the blight, can the government use it?"

"Most of the risk was to myself, and look at the damage done to the drug trade, I think that offsets any harm done. Also, the blight doesn't work I can assure you, though in the future it might. The DNA mapping I did, does work and the University has it up and working again. It could do a lot of good." Adrian answered.

"Why did you put all the money in his account? Why didn't you keep some?"

"Because there could be no discrepancies, it had to be all there, or the American government would've kept looking for it."

"Then what did you get out of all this?" Brett asked thinking Emma and the others must be getting something, Emma definitely looked happy.

"I didn't say we didn't take anything from his account. Before we put the two amounts in, we withdrew a billion dollars. He still had more than seven hundred million in the account." Adrian smiled. It took Brett a moment to take in what he'd said.

"They'll find out you've got it Adrian surely there's records?"

"Before Senator Jefferies was killed in a freak car accident, he'd transferred his money through a dozen accounts. The American government has seised it now, and are quite happy with the money they found there. I can assure you, no one cares about any of us."

"I don't know what to say," Brett admitted overwhelmed by the day's advents.

"Do you want your ten percent?" Adrian asked as the others chuckling, watching his reaction. Brett sat there thinking of another question, nothing came.

"Of course I do. Although I still think you could've told me." He smiled, as the others exploded with merriment at his acceptance of the situation. After Brett had come to terms with what they'd done, he settled down as their plane taxied onto the runway.

"Where are we going too?" Brett asked.

"Back home to Byron in Australia. It's about time we all settled down." Robbo answered sitting down next to Emma grabbing her leg, making her giggle.

"What about my passport shouldn't I see someone before I leave New Zealand?" Brett enquired.

"It's been taken care of. You're officially doing your job now, protecting a rich Australian." Adrian answered smiling.

As everyone strapped in, Linda seated herself next to Brett.

"I'm so sorry about all this Brett. I wanted to tell you several times, I just knew you wouldn't have gone along with it."

"You're right I wouldn't have. Despite what you all achieved, it could have gone south, and one of you might've paid the price.

"You've got to admit, this will certainly change your life?"

"The money aside, finding out that Corteze was behind the contract that killed Susan, was worth taking any risk. Even without the money, I'd have been happy knowing that."

"What happens now with us?" Linda whispered.

"I'm still unsure that the government will do nothing about the money. That aside, we'll still take our share and enjoy life, without the booze." Brett answered kissing Linda.

FBI HEADQUARTERS WASHINGTON

Director Sharn Davison looked around at her new office. The President had as she predicted, named a woman to head up the FBI. As expected she got the job as a reward for the total destruction of several drug cartels. Smiling, she thought of how many arseholes she'd had to sleep with to get this job.

"It should have been mine by ability." She said to herself, as she sat down at the director's desk. Adjusting the chair to suit herself she looked out the window over Washington, before going over the morning reports.

'It's too bad Brett couldn't be here' she thought, missing the first man who'd surprised her in being honourable. She had been worried by his fall after being sacked, and one of her first assignments for her new assistant had been to secretly find out where he was. On cue, Dan Crawford her assistant entered her office.

Dan had worked at the University for both Crammer and later Brett during the search for Adrian. He was happily married and honest, both things which Sharn wanted in an assistant.

"How'd the search on Brett Heckle go?" Sharn asked. At first, Dan seemed reluctant to answer, in the end, he showed Sharn a picture of Brett and Adrian with two women, sitting at a hotel overlooking a beach. Sharn picked up the photo seeing Adrian looked in good health and happy. He also seemed fully recovered something the experts had assured them wouldn't occur. Yet there he was, appearing quite normal, laughing at some joke Brett had told.

"It seems Adrian had a miracle recovery?"

"Yes, they all seem to be doing well," Dan answered.

"Where was the photo taken?"

"Byron Bay in Australia."

"Who are the two women?"

"One's an Australian citizen with a Japanese father. The others an American named Linda Brighton. Linda worked at the bar where Adrian was kidnapped from. The other woman named Kim was also in America at the time of Adrian's kidnapping." Dan pointed out.

"Bit of a coincidence. Have they all come into any money lately? They seem to be enjoying themselves."

"That's hard to find out. It seems Adrian and several of his friends, including Brett and the two women, have Swiss bank accounts. I did a little digging; I'd say between them they have several hundred million."

"Makes you wonder where it all came from doesn't it? What do you think we should do about it, Dan?"

"I'm not the boss, you are. As for me, next holiday break, I'm taking my family to Australia to stay with a good friend."

"Well, the President did order that no one was to go near either Adrian or Brett. I think we should follow orders, don't you?" She grinned. Dan was just about to answer when Sharn's phone started ringing. Picking it up, he asked who was calling. Seeing him tense up, Sharn knew it was someone important.

"It's the President," Dan answered, as Sharn nodding, gestured for him to leave. "What about this?" Dan whispered, indicating the file on Brett and Adrian.

"Shred it," Sharn said softly, as Dan smiling left.

"Good morning Mr President. What can I do for you?" Sharn asked smiling, still thinking about Brett.

"I have a couple of problems. I thought you could come over tonight and over dinner, we could discuss them."

"Of course Mr President, I'll be there at six."

"No, make it eight. My wife leaves for Camp David at seven. We can have the evening alone."

"Of course Mr President, eight it is."

"And call me Bill from now on Sharn. See you tonight". He chuckled, hanging up. Staring at the phone, Sharn fumed. Slamming it back down onto the desk, she got up walking to the window. All the sexual bullshit she'd put up with to get to the top and still she was being used. Thinking again about Brett, she smiled, making a decision. She decided to leave work early and go shopping.

Arriving at one of her favourite boutiques she bought a special outfit for her night with the President. She'd also included an extremely brief matching set of silk lingerie. The President she smiled would never forget this night and to make sure, she decided to record it all.

"If Adrian and Brett can retire with the help of this administration, so can I." She giggled, deciding on holiday in Australia as well.

THE END